Books by Olivia Gates

Harlequin Desire

The Sarantos Secret Baby #2080
**To Touch a Sheikh #2103*
A Secret Birthright #2136
ΩThe Sheikh's Redemption #2165
ΩThe Sheikh's Claim #2183
ΩThe Sheikh's Destiny #2201
§Temporarily His Princess #2231
§Conveniently His Princess #2255

*Throne of Judar
ΔThe Castaldini Crown
**Pride of Zohayd
ΩDesert Knights
§Married by Royal Decree

Other titles by this author
available in ebook format.

Silhouette Desire

The Desert Lord's Baby #1872
The Desert Lord's Bride #1884
The Desert King #1896
ΔThe Once and Future Prince #19██
ΔThe Prodigal Prince's S█████
ΔThe Illegitimate King ████
Billionaire, M.D. #200█
In Too Deep #2025
"The Sheikh's Bargain█
**To Tame a Sheikh #2050█
**To Tempt a Sheikh #2069

OLIVIA GATES

has always pursued creative passions such as singing and handicrafts. She still does, but only one of her passions grew gratifying enough, consuming enough, to become an ongoing career—writing.

She is most fulfilled when she is creating worlds and conflicts for her characters, then exploring and untangling them bit by bit, sharing her protagonists' every heart-wrenching heartache and hope, their every heart-pounding doubt and trial, until she leads them to an indisputably earned and gloriously satisfying happy ending.

When she's not writing, she is a doctor, a wife to her own alpha male and a mother to one brilliant girl and one demanding Angora cat. Visit Olivia at www.oliviagates.com.

To my family and friends, who give me all I need...
love, understanding, encouragement and space,
to keep on writing...and enjoying it. Love you all.

In Moments, She Drove Away With A Screech.

He stood watching her backlights flash red as she hit the brakes at the garage's exit, the adrenaline of exhilaration flooding his system.

She'd really done it. Something no other woman, no other person, had ever done. She'd turned him down. No. More. She'd *rebuffed* him. And then some.

Well. There was only one thing he could do now.

Give chase.

* * *

Conveniently His Princess is a
Married by Royal Decree novel:
When the king commands, they say "I do!"

* * *

If you're on Twitter,
tell us what you think of Harlequin Desire!
#harlequindesire

Dear Reader,

When I first met Aram Nazaryan in the first book of the Pride of Zohayd trilogy, *To Tame A Sheikh,* he told me he had a heart that had been lonely all his life, the deepest need for belonging among my heroes...*but* that he'd long given up on the hope that he'd ever have his heart filled, or would ever belong with anyone, or anywhere.

Then his best friend and brother-in-law, Prince Shaheen Aal Shalaan, offered him what would provide him with a family and a return to the one place he'd ever called home...Zohayd.

I winced as I heard the offer, for I knew this "Marry a Princess to Become Royal" snag would make Aram refuse. He wasn't a man who would marry for convenience, and certainly not "Kanza The Monster."

He did refuse, and I thought all was lost...until he met said "Monster"... and she proceeded to turn him inside out and his world upside down.

It was a delight to go on this roller-coaster ride with Aram and Kanza as they developed a unique-to-my-heroes-and-heroines connection. Their feelings developed from antagonism to camaraderie, then from close friendship to the deepest reaches of passion. I was heartbroken along with them when everything seemed to be destroyed beyond repair. I hope you will feel as powerfully about their relationship as I do.

I love to hear from readers, so please visit my website for my latest news at www.oliviagates.com, email me at oliviagates@gmail.com, and connect with me on Facebook, www.facebook.com/oliviagatesauthor, on Goodreads, www.goodreads.com/author/show/405461.Olivia_Gates and on Twitter, @OliviaGates.

Thanks for reading!

Olivia

CONVENIENTLY
HIS PRINCESS

—

OLIVIA GATES

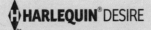

Recycling programs
for this product may
not exist in your area.

ISBN-13: 978-0-373-73268-5

CONVENIENTLY HIS PRINCESS

Printed in U.S.A.

One

"You want me to marry Kanza the Monster?"

Aram Nazaryan winced at the loudness of his own voice.

Not that anyone could blame him for going off like that. Shaheen Aal Shalaan had made some unacceptable requests in his time, but *this* one warranted a description not yet coined by any language he knew. And he knew four.

But the transformation of his best and only friend into a meddling mother hen had been steadily progressing from ignorable to untenable for the past three years. It seemed that the happier Shaheen became with Aram's kid sister Johara after they had miraculously reunited and gotten married, the more sorry for Aram he became and the more he intensified his efforts to get his brother-in-law to change what he called his "unlife."

And to think he'd still been gullible enough to believe that Shaheen had dropped by his office for a simple visit. Ten minutes into the chitchat, he'd carpet bombed him with emotional blackmail.

He'd started by abandoning all subtlety about enticing him to go back to Zohayd, asking him point-blank to come *home*.

Annoyed into equal bluntness, he'd finally retorted that Zohayd was Shaheen's home, not his, and he wouldn't go back there to be the family's seventh wheel, when Shaheen and Johara's second baby arrived.

Shaheen had only upped the ante of his persistence. To prove that he'd have a vital role and a full life in Zohayd, he'd offered him his job. He'd actually asked him to become Zohayd's freaking minister of economy!

Thinking that Shaheen was pulling his leg, he'd at first laughed. What else could it be but a joke when only a royal Zohaydan could assume that role, and the last time Aram checked, he was a French-Armenian American?

Shaheen, regretfully, hadn't sprouted a sense of humor. What he had was a harebrained plan of how Aram could *become* a royal Zohaydan. By marrying a Zohaydan princess.

Before he could bite Shaheen's head off for that suggestion, his brother-in-law had hit him with the identity of the candidate he thought *perfect* for him. And *that* had been the last straw.

Aram shot his friend an incredulous look when Shaheen rose to face him. "Has conjugal bliss finally fried your brain, Shaheen? There's no way I'm marrying that monster."

In response, Shaheen reeled back his flabbergasted expression, adjusting it to a neutral one. "I don't know where you got that name. The Kanza I know is certainly no monster."

"Then there are two different Kanzas. The one I know, Kanza Aal Ajmaan, the princess from a maternal branch of your royal family, has earned that name and then some."

Shaheen's gaze became cautious, as if he were dealing with a madman. "There's only one Kanza...and she is delightful."

"Delightful?" A spectacular snort accompanied that exclamation. "But let's say I go along with your delusion and agree that she is Miss Congeniality herself. Are you out of your mind even suggesting her to me? She's a kid!"

It was Shaheen's turn to snort. "She's almost thirty."

"Wha…? No way. The last time I saw her she was somewhere around eighteen."

"Yes. And that was over ten years ago."

Had it really been that long? A quick calculation said it had been, since he'd last seen her at that fateful ball, days before he'd left Zohayd.

He waved the realization away. "Whatever. The eleven or twelve years between us sure hasn't shrunk by time."

"I'm eight years older than Johara. Three or four years' more age difference might have been a big deal back then, but it's no longer a concern at your respective ages now."

"That may be your opinion, but I…" He stopped, huffed a laugh, shaking his finger at Shaheen. "Oh, no, you don't. You're not dragging me into discussing her as if she's actually a possibility. She's a monster, I'm telling you."

"And I'm telling you she's no such thing."

"Okay, let's go into details, shall we? The Kanza I knew was a dour, sullen creature who sent people scurrying in the opposite direction just by glaring at them. In fact, every time she looked my way, I thought I'd find two holes drilled into me wherever her gaze landed, fuming black, billowing smoke."

Shaheen whistled. "Quite the image. I see she made quite an impression on you, if after over ten years you still recall her with such vividness and her very memory still incites such intense reactions."

"Intense *unfavorable* reactions." He grunted in disgust. "It's appalling enough that you're suggesting this marriage of convenience at all but to recommend the one…creature who ever creeped the hell out of me?"

"Creeped?" Shaheen tutted. "Don't you think you're going overboard here?"

He scowled, his pesky sense of fairness rearing its head. "Okay, so perhaps *creeped* is not the right word. She just… disturbed me. *She* is disturbed. Do you know that horror once went around with purple hair, green full-body paint and pink contact lenses? Another time she went total albino rabbit with white hair and red eyes. The last time I saw her she had blue hair and zombie makeup. *That* was downright creepy."

Shaheen's smile became that of an adult coddling an unreasonable child. "What, apart from weird hair and eye color and makeup experimentation, do you have against her?"

"The way she used to mutter my name, as if she was casting a curse. I always had the impression she had some… goblin living inside her wisp of a body."

Shaheen shoved his hands inside his pockets, the image of complacency. "Sounds like she's exactly what you need. You could certainly use someone that potent to thaw you out of the deep freeze you've been stuck in for around two decades now."

"Why don't I just go stick myself in an incinerator? It would handle that deep freeze much more effectively and far less painfully."

Shaheen only gave him the forbearing, compassionate look of a man who knew such deep contentment and fulfillment and was willing to take anything from his poor, unfortunate friend with the barren life.

"Quit it with the pitying look, Shaheen. My temperature is fine. It's how I am now.… It's called growing up."

"If only. Johara feels your coldness. I feel it. Your parents are frantic, believing they'd done that to you when you were forced to remain with your father in Zohayd at the expense of your own life."

"Nobody forced me to do anything. I chose to stay with Father because he wouldn't have survived alone after his breakup with Mother."

"And when they eventually found their way back to each other, you'd already sacrificed your own desires and ambitions and swerved from your own planned path to support your family, and you've never been able to correct your course. Now you're still trapped on the outside, watching the rest of us live our lives from that solitude of yours."

Aram glowered at Shaheen. He was happy, incredibly so, for his mother and father. For his sister and best friend. But when they kept shoving his so-called solitude in his face, he felt nothing endearing toward any of them. Their solicitude only chafed when he knew he couldn't do anything about it.

"I made my own choices, so there's nothing for anyone to feel guilty about. The solitude you lament suits me just fine. So put your minds the hell at ease and leave me be."

"I'll be happy to, right after you give my proposition serious consideration and not dismiss it out of hand."

"Said proposition deserves nothing else."

"Give me one good reason it does. Citing things about Kanza that are ten years outdated doesn't count."

"How about an updated one? If she's twenty-eight—"

"She'll be twenty-nine in a few months."

"And she hasn't married yet—I assume no poor man has taken her off the shelf only to drop her back there like a burning coal and run into the horizon screaming?"

Shaheen's pursed lips were the essence of disapproval. "No, she hasn't been married or even engaged."

He smirked in self-satisfaction at the accuracy of his projections. "At her age, by Zohaydan standards, she's already long fossilized."

"How gallant of you, Aram. I thought you were a progressive man who's against all backward ideas, including ageism. I never dreamed you'd hold a woman's age against her in anything, let alone in her suitability for marriage."

"You know I don't subscribe to any of that crap. What I'm saying is if she is a Zohaydan woman, and a princess, who didn't get approached by a man for that long, it is proof that she is generally viewed as incompatible with human life."

"The exact same thing could be said about you."

Throwing his hands up in exasperation, he landed them on his friend's shoulders. "Listen carefully, Shaheen, because I'll say this once, and we will not speak of this again. I will not get married. Not to become Zohaydan and become your minister of economy, not for any other reason. If you really need my help, I'll gladly offer you and Zohayd my services."

Shaheen, who had clearly anticipated this as one of Aram's answers, was ready with his rebuttal. "The level of involvement needed has to be full-time, with you taking the top job and living in Zohayd."

"I have my own business…"

"Which you've set up so ingeniously and have trained your deputies so thoroughly you only need to supervise operations from afar for it to continue on its current trajectory of phenomenal success. This level of efficiency, this uncanny ability to employ the right people and to get the best out of them is exactly what I need you to do for Zohayd."

"*You* haven't been working the job full-time," he pointed out.

"Only because my father has been helping me since he abdicated. But now he's retreating from public life completely. Even with his help, I've been torn between my family, my business and the ministry. Now we have another baby on the way and family time will only increase. And Johara is becoming more involved in humanitarian projects that require my attention, as well. I simply can't find a way to juggle it all if I remain minister."

He narrowed his eyes at Shaheen. "So I should sacrifice my own life to smooth out yours?"

"You'd be sacrificing nothing. Your business will continue as always, you'd be the best minister of economy humanly possible, a position you'd revel in, and you'll get a family…something I know you have always longed for."

Yeah. He was the only male he knew who'd planned at

sixteen that he'd get married by eighteen, have half a dozen kids, pick one place and one job and grow deep, deep roots.

And here he was, forty, alone and rootless.

How had that happened?

Which was the rhetorical question to end all rhetorical questions. He knew just how.

"What I longed for and what I am equipped for are poles apart, Shaheen. I've long come to terms with the fact that I'm never getting married, never having a family. This might be unimaginable to you in your state of familial nirvana, but not everyone is made for wedded bliss. Given the number of broken homes worldwide, I'd say those who are equipped for it are a minority. I happen to be one of the majority, but I happen to be at peace with it."

It was Shaheen who took him by the shoulders now. "I believed the exact same thing about myself before Johara found me again. Now look at me…ecstatically united with the one right person."

Aram bit back a comment that would take this argument into an unending loop. That it was Shaheen and Johara's marriage that had shattered any delusions he'd entertained that he could ever get married himself.

What they had together—this total commitment, trust, friendship and passion—was what he'd always dreamed of. Their example had made him certain that if he couldn't have that—and he didn't entertain the least hope he'd ever have it—then he couldn't settle for anything less.

Evidently worried that Aram had stopped arguing, Shaheen rushed to add, "I'm not asking you to get married tomorrow, Aram. I'm just asking you to consider the possibility."

"I don't need to. I have been and will always remain perfectly fine on my own."

Eager to put an abrupt end to this latest bout of emotional wrestling—the worst he'd had so far with Shaheen—he started to turn around, but his friend held him back.

He leveled fed-up eyes on Shaheen. *"Now what?"*

"You look like hell."

He felt like it, too. As for how he looked, during nec-essary self-maintenance he'd indeed been seeing a frayed edition of the self he remembered.

Seemed hitting forty did hit a man hard.

A huff of deprecation escaped him. "Why, thanks, Sha-heen. You were always such a sweet talker."

"I'm telling it as it is, Aram. You're working yourself into the ground…and if you think I'm blunt, it's nothing com-pared to what Amjad said when he last saw you."

Amjad, the king of Zohayd, Shaheen's oldest brother. The Mad Prince turned the Crazy King. And one of the biggest jerks in human history.

Aram exhaled in disgust. "I was right there when he rel-ished the fact that I looked 'like something the cat dragged in, chewed up and barfed.' But thanks for bringing up that royal pain. I didn't even factor him in my refusal. But even if I considered the job offer/marriage package the oppor-tunity of a lifetime, I'd still turn it down flat because it would bring me in contact with *him.* I can't believe you're actually asking me to become a minister in that inhuman affliction's cabinet."

Shaheen grinned at his diatribe. "You'll work with me, not him."

"No, I won't. Give it up, already."

Shaheen looked unsatisfied and tried again. "About Kanza…"

A memory burst in his head. He couldn't believe it hadn't come to him before. "Yes, about her and about abomina-tions for older siblings. You didn't only pick Kanza the Monster for my best match but the half sister of the Fury herself, Maysoon."

"I hoped you'd forgotten about her. But I guess that was asking too much." Wryness twisted Shaheen's lips. "May-soon was a tad…temperamental."

"A tad?" he scoffed. "She was a raging basket case. I barely escaped her in one piece."

And she'd been the reason that he'd had to leave Zohayd and his father behind. The reason he'd had to abandon his dream of ever making a home there.

"Kanza is her extreme opposite, anyway."

"You got that right. While Maysoon was a stunning if unstable harpy, Kanza was an off-putting miscreant."

"I diametrically differ with your evaluation of Kanza. While I know she may not be…sophisticated like her womenfolk, Kanza's very unpretentiousness makes me like her far more. Even if you don't consider those virtues exciting, they would actually make her a more suitable wife for you."

Aram lifted a sarcastic brow. "You figure?"

"I do. It would make her safe and steady, not like the fickle, demanding women you're used to."

"You're only making your argument even more inadmissible, Shaheen. Even if I wanted this, and I consider almost anything admissible in achieving my objectives, I would draw the line at exploiting the mousy, unworldly spinster you're painting her to be."

"Who says there'd be any exploitation? You might be a pain in the neck that rivals even Amjad sometimes but you're one of the most coveted eligible bachelors in the world. Kanza would probably jump at the opportunity to be your wife."

Maybe. Probably. Still…

"No, Shaheen. And that's final."

The forcefulness he'd injected into his voice seemed to finally get to Shaheen, who looked at him with that drop-it-now-to-attack-another-day expression that he knew all too well.

Aram clamped his friend's arm, dragging him to the door. "Now go home, Shaheen. Kiss Johara and Gharam for me."

Shaheen still resisted being shoved out. "Just assess the

situation like you do any other business proposition before you make a decision either way."

Aram groaned. Shaheen was one dogged son of a king. "I've already made a decision, Shaheen, so give it a rest."

Before he finally walked away, Shaheen gave him that unfazed smile of his that eloquently said he wouldn't.

Resigned that he hadn't heard the last of this, Aram closed the door after him with a decisive click.

The moment he did, his shoulders slumped as his feet dragged to the couch. Throwing himself down on it, he decided to spend yet another night there. No need for him to go "home." Since he didn't have one anyway.

But as he stretched out and closed his eyes, his meeting with Shaheen revolved in his mind in a nonstop loop.

He might have sent Shaheen on his way with an adamant refusal, but it wasn't that easy to suppress his own temptation.

Shaheen's previous persuasions hadn't even given him pause. After all, there had been nothing for him to do in Zohayd except be with his family, who had their priorities—of which he wasn't one. But now that Shaheen was dangling that job offer in front of him, he could actually visualize a real future there.

He'd given Zohayd's economy constant thought when he'd lived there, had studied it and planned to make it his life's work. Now, as if Shaheen had been privy to all that, he was offering him the very position where he could utilize all his talents and expertise and put his plans into action.

Then came that one snag in what could have been a once-in-a-lifetime opportunity.

The get-married-to-become-Zohaydan one.

But…should it be a snag? Maybe convenience was the one way he *could* get married. And since he didn't want to get married for real, perhaps Shaheen's candidate *was* exactly what he needed.

Her family was royal but not too high up on the tree of

royalty as to be too lofty, and their fortune was nowhere near his billionaire status. Maybe as Shaheen had suggested, she'd give him the status he needed, luxuriate in the boost in wealth he'd provide and stay out of his hair.

He found himself standing before the wall-to-wall mirror in the bathroom. He didn't know how he'd gotten there. Meeting his own eyes jogged him out of the preposterous trajectory of his thoughts.

He winced at himself. Shaheen had played him but good. He'd actually made him consider the impossible.

And it was impossible. Being in Zohayd, the only place that had been home to him, being with his family, being Zohayd's minister of economy were nice fantasies.

And they would remain just that.

Miraculously, Shaheen hadn't pursued the subject further.

Wonders would never cease, it seemed.

The only thing he'd brought up in the past two weeks had been an invitation to a party he and Johara were holding in their New York penthouse tonight. An invitation he'd declined.

He was driving to the hotel where he "lived," musing over Shaheen dropping the subject, wrestling with this ridiculously perverse sense of disappointment, when his phone rang. Johara.

He pressed the Bluetooth button and her voice poured its warmth over the crystal-clear connection.

"Aram, please tell me you're not working or sleeping."

He barely caught back a groan. This must be about the party, and he'd hate refusing her to her ears. It was an actual physical pain being unable to give Johara whatever she wanted. Since the moment she'd been born, he'd been a *khaatem f'esba'ha,* or "a ring on her finger," as they said in Zohayd. He was lucky that she was part angel or she would have used him as her rattle toy through life.

He prayed she wouldn't exercise her power over him, make it impossible for him to turn down the invitation again. He was at an all-time low, wasn't in any condition to be exposed to her and Shaheen's happiness.

He imbued his voice with the smile that only Johara could generate inside him no matter what. "I'm driving back to the hotel, sweetheart. Are you almost ready for your party?"

"Oh, I am, but…are you already there? If you are, don't bother. I'll think of something else."

He frowned. "What is this all about, Johara?"

Sounding apologetic, she sighed. "There's a very important file that one of my guests gave me to read, and we'd planned to discuss it at the party. Unfortunately, I forgot it back in my office at Shaheen's building, and I can't leave now. So I was wondering if you could go get the file and bring it here to me?" She hesitated. "I'm sorry to take you out of your way and I promise not to try to persuade you to stay at the party, but I can't trust anyone else with the pass codes to my filing cabinets."

"You know you can ask me anything at all, anytime."

"Anything but come to the party, huh?" He started to recite the rehearsed excuse he'd given Shaheen, and she interjected, "But Shaheen told me you did look like you needed an early night, so I totally understand. And it's not as if I could have enjoyed your company anyway, since we've invited a few dozen people and I'll be flitting all over playing hostess."

He let out a sigh of relief for her letting him off the hook, looking forward to seeing them yet having the excuse to keep the visit to the brevity he could withstand tonight.

"Tell me what to look for."

Twenty minutes later, Aram was striding across the top floor of Shaheen's skyscraper.

As he entered Johara's company headquarters, he

frowned. The door to her assistants' office, which led to hers, was open. Weird.

Deciding that it must have been a rare oversight in their haste to attend Johara and Shaheen's soiree, he walked in and found the door to his sister's private office also ajar. Before he could process this new information, a slam reverberated through him.

He froze, his senses on high alert. Not that it took any effort to pinpoint the source of the noise. The racket that followed was unmistakable in direction and nature. Someone was inside Johara's office and was turning it upside down.

Thief was the first thing that jumped into his mind.

But no. There was no way anyone could have bypassed security. Except someone the guards knew. Maybe one of Johara's assistants was in there looking for the file she'd asked him for? But she had been clear she hadn't trusted anyone else with her personal pass codes. So could one of her employees be trying to break into her files?

No, again. He trusted his gut feelings, and he knew Johara had chosen her people well.

Then perhaps someone who worked for Shaheen was trying to steal classified info only she as his wife would be privy to?

Maybe. Calling the guards was the logical next step, anyway. But if he'd jumped to conclusions it could cause unnecessary fright and embarrassment to whomever was inside. He should take a look before he made up his mind how to proceed.

He neared the door in soundless steps, not that the person inside would have heard a marching band. A bulldozer wouldn't have caused more commotion than that intruder. That alone was just cause to give whomever it was a bit of a scare.

Peeping inside, he primed himself for a confrontation if need be. The next moment, everything in his mind emptied.

It was a woman. Young, slight, wiry. With the thickest

mane of hair he'd ever seen flying after her like dark flames as she crashed about Johara's office. And she didn't look in the least worried she'd be caught in the act.

Without making a conscious decision, he found himself striding right in.

Then he heard himself saying, "Why don't you fill me in on what you're looking for?"

The woman jumped in the air. She was so light, her movement so vertical, so high, it triggered an exaggerated image in his mind of a cartoon character jumping out of her skin in fright. It almost forced a laugh from his lips at its absurdity yet its appropriateness for this brownie.

The laugh dissolved into a smile that hadn't touched his lips in far too long as she turned to him.

He watched her, feeling as if time was decelerating, like one of those slow-motion movie sequences that signified a momentous event.

He heard himself again, amusement soaking his drawl. "I hear that while searching for something that evidently elusive, two sets of hands and eyes, not to mention two brains, are better than one."

With his last word, she was facing him. And though her face was a canvas of shock, and he could tell from her shapeless black shirt and pants that the tiny sprite was unarmed, it felt as if he'd gotten a kick in his gut.

And that was before her startled expression faded, before those fierce, dark eyes flayed a layer off his skin and her husky voice burned down his nerve endings.

"I should have known the unfortunate event of tripping into your presence was a territorial hazard around this place. So what brings you to your poor sister's office while she's not around? Is no one safe from the raids of The Pirate?"

Two

Aram stared at the slight creature who faced him across the elegant office, radiating the impact of a miniature force of nature, and one thing reverberating through his mind.

She'd recognized him on the spot.

No. More than that. She *knew* him. At least knew *of* him.

She'd called him "The Pirate." The persona, or rather the caricature of him that distasteful tabloids, scorned women and disgruntled business rivals had popularized.

She seemed to be waiting for him to make a comeback to her opening salvo.

A charge of electricity forked up his spine, then all the way up to his lips, spreading them wider. "So I'm The Pirate. And what do you answer to? The Tornado? The Hurricane? You did tear through Johara's office with the comparative havoc of one. Or do you simply go with The Burglar? A very messy, noisy, reckless one at that?"

She tilted her head, sending her masses of glossy curls tumbling over one slim shoulder. He could swear he heard them tutting in sarcastic vexation that echoed the expression on her elfin face.

It also poured into her voice, its timbre causing something inside his rib cage to rev. "So are you going to stand there like the behemoth that you are blocking my escape route and sucking all oxygen from the room into that ridiculously massive chest of yours, or are you going to give a fellow thief a hand?"

His lips twitched, every word out of hers another zap lashing through his nerves. "Now, how is it fair that I assist you in your heist without even having the privilege of knowing who I'm going to be indicted with when we're caught? Or are formal introductions not even necessary? Perhaps your spritely self plans on disappearing into the night, leaving me behind to take the fall?"

Her stare froze on him for several long seconds before she suddenly tossed her hair back with a careless hand. "Oh, right…I remember now. Sorry for that. I guess having you materialize behind me like some genie surprised me so much it took me a while to reboot and access my memory banks."

He blinked, then frowned. Was she the one who'd stopped making sense, or had his mind finally stopped functioning? It *had* been increasingly glitch riddled of late. He had been teetering on the brink of some breakdown for a long time now, and he'd thought it was only a matter of time before the chasm running through his being became complete.

So had his psyche picked now of all times to hit rock bottom? But why *now,* when he'd finally found someone to jog him out of his apathy, even if temporarily; someone he actually couldn't predict?

Maybe he'd blacked out or something, missed something she'd said that would make her last words make sense.

He cleared his throat. "Uh…come again?"

Her fed-up expression deepened. "I momentarily forgot how you got your nickname, and that you continue to live down to it, and then some."

Though the jump in continuity still baffled him, he went along. "Oh? I'm very much interested in hearing your dissection of my character. Knowing how another criminal mastermind perceives me would no doubt help me perfect my M.O."

One of those dense, slanting eyebrows rose. "Invoking the code of dishonor among thieves? Sure, why not? I'm charitable like that with fellow crooks." That obsidian gaze poured mockery over him. "Let's see. You earned your moniker after building a reputation of treating other sentient beings like commodities to be pillaged then tossed aside once their benefit is depleted. But you reserve an added insult and injury to those who suffer the terrible misfortune of being exposed to you on a personal level, as you reward those hapless people by deleting them from you mind. So, if you're seeking my counsel about enhancing your performance, my opinion is that you can't improve on your M.O. of perfectly efficient cruelty."

Her scathing portrayal *was* the image that had been painted of him in the business world and by the women he'd kept away by whatever measures necessary.

When his actions had been exaggerated or misinterpreted and that ruthless reputation had begun to be established, he'd never tried to adjust it. On the contrary, he'd let it become entrenched, since that perceived cold-bloodedness did endow him with a power nothing else could. Not to mention that it supplied him with peace of mind he couldn't have bought if he'd projected a more approachable persona. This one did keep the world at bay.

But the only actual accuracy in her summation was the personal interactions bit. He didn't crowd his recollections with the mundane details of anyone who hadn't proved worth his while. Only major incidents remained in his memory—if stripped from any emotional impact they might have had.

But…wait a minute. Inquiring about her identity had triggered this caustic commentary in the first place. Was she obliquely saying that he didn't remember *her,* when he should?

That was just not possible. How would he have ever forgotten those eyes that could reduce a man to ashes at thirty paces, or that tongue that could shred him to ribbons, or that wit that could weave those ribbons into the hand basket to send him to hell in?

No way. If he'd ever as much as exchanged a few words with her, not only would he have remembered, he would probably have borne the marks of every one. After mere minutes of being exposed to her, he felt her eyes and tongue had left no part of him unscathed.

And he was loving it.

God, to be reveling in this, he must be sicker than he'd thought of all the fawning he got from everyone else—especially women. Though he knew *that* had never been for *him.* During his stint in Zohayd, it had been his exotic looks but mainly his closeness to the royal family that had incited the relentless pursuit of women there. After he'd become a millionaire, then a billionaire... Well, status and wealth were irresistible magnets to almost everyone.

That made being slammed with such downright derision unprecedented. He doubted if he would have accepted it from anyone else, though. But from this enigma, he was outright relishing it.

Wanting to incite even more of her verbal insults, he gave her a bow of mock gratitude. "Your testimony of dishonor honors me, and your maligning warms my stone-cold heart."

Both her eyebrows shot up this time. "You have one? I thought your species didn't come equipped with those superfluous organs."

His grin widened. "I do have a rudimentary thing somewhere."

"Like an appendix?" A short, derogatory sound purred in the back of her throat. "Something that could be excised and you'd probably function better without? Wonder why you didn't have it electively removed. It must be festering in there."

As if compelled, he moved away from the door, needing a closer look at this being he'd never seen the likes of before. He kept drawing nearer as she stood her ground, her glare one that could have stopped an attacking horde.

It only made getting even closer imperative. He stopped only when he was three feet away, peering down at this diminutive woman who was a good foot or more shorter than he was yet feeling as if he was standing nose to nose with an equal.

"Don't worry," he finally said, answering her last dig. "There is no reason for surgical intervention. It has long since shriveled and calcified. But thank you from the bottom of my vestigial heart for the concern. And for the counsel. It's indeed reassuring to have such a merciless authority confirm that I'm doing the wrong thing so right."

He waited for her ricocheting blitz, anticipation rising. Instead, she seared him with an incinerating glance before seeming to delete *him* from her mind as she resumed her search.

By now he knew for certain that she wasn't here to do anything behind Johara's back. Even when she'd readily engaged him in the "thieves in the night" scenario he'd initiated, and rifling through the very cabinets he himself was here to search...

It suddenly hit him, right in the solar plexus, who this tempest in human form was.

It was *her*.

Kanza. Kanza Aal Ajmaan.

Unable to blink, to breathe, he stood staring at her as she kept transferring files from the cabinets, plopping them down on Johara's desk before attacking them with a speed and focus that once again flooded his mind's eye with images of hilarious cartoon characters. He had no clue how he'd even recognized her. Just as she'd accused him, his memories of the Kanza he'd known over ten years ago had been stripped of any specifics.

All he could recall of the fierce and fearsome teenager she'd been, apart from the caricature he'd painted for Shaheen of her atrocious fashion style and the weird, bordering-on-repulsive things she'd done with her hair and eyes, was that it had felt as if something ancient had been inhabiting that younger-than-her-age body.

A decade later, she still seemed more youthful than her chronological age, yet packed the wallop of this same primal force. But that was where the resemblance ended.

The Mad Hatter and Wicked Witch clothes and makeup and extraterrestrial hair, contact lenses and body paint were gone now. From the nondescript black clothes and the white sneakers that clashed with them, to the face scrubbed clean of any enhancements, to the thick, untamed mahogany tresses that didn't seem to have met a stylist since he'd last seen her, she had gone all the way in the other direction.

Though in an opposite way to her former self, she was still the antithesis of all the svelte, stylish women who'd ever entered his orbit, starting with her half sisters. Where they'd been overtly feminine and flaunting their assets, she made no effort whatsoever to maximize any attributes she might have. Not that she had much to work with. She was small, almost boyish. The only big thing about her was her hair. And eyes. Those were enormous. Everything else was tiny.

But that was when he analyzed her looks clinically. But when he experienced them with the influence of the being they housed, the spirit that animated them…that was when his entire perception changed. The pattern of her features, the shape of her lips, the sweep of her lashes, the energy of her movements… Everything about her evolved into something totally different, making her something far more interesting than pretty.

Singular. Compelling.

And the most singular and compelling thing about her was those night eyes that had burned to ashes any preformed ideas of what made a woman worthy of a second glance, let alone constant staring.

Though he was still staring after she'd deprived him of their contact, he *was* glad to be relieved of their all-seeing scrutiny. He needed respite to process finding her here.

How could Shaheen bring her up a couple of weeks ago only for him to stumble on her here of all places when he hadn't crossed paths with her in ten years? This was too much of a coincidence. Which meant…

It wasn't one. Johara had set him up.

Another realization hit simultaneously.

Kanza seemed to be here running his same errand. Evidently Johara had set her up, too.

God. He was growing duller by the day. How could he have even thought Shaheen wouldn't share this with Johara, the woman where half his soul resided? How hadn't he picked up on Johara's knowledge or intentions?

Not that those two coconspirators were important now. The only relevant thing here was Kanza.

Had she realized the setup once he'd walked through that door? Was that why she'd reacted so cuttingly to his appearance? Did she take exception to Johara's matchmaking, and that was her way of telling her, and him, "Hell, no!"?

If this was the truth, then that made her even more interesting than he'd originally thought. It wasn't conceit, but as Shaheen had said, in the marriage market, he was about as big a catch as an eligible bachelor got. He couldn't imagine any woman would be averse to the idea of being his wife— if only for his status and wealth. Even his reputation was an irresistible lure in that arena. If women thought they had access, it only made him more of a challenge, a dangerous bad boy each dreamed she'd be the one to tame.

But if Kanza was so immune to his assets, so opposed

to exploring his possibility as a groom, that alone made her worthy of in-depth investigation.

Not that *he* was even considering Shaheen and Johara's neat little plan. But he *was* more intrigued by the moment by this…entity they'd gotten it into their minds was perfect for him.

Suddenly, said entity looked up from the files, transfixed him in the crosshairs of her fiercest glare yet. "Don't just stand there and pose. Come do something more useful than look pretty." When she saw his eyebrows shoot up, her lips twisted. "What? You take exception to being called pretty?"

He opened his mouth to answer, and her impatient gesture closed it for him, had him hurrying next to her where she foisted a pile of files on him and instructed him to look for the very file Johara had sent him here to retrieve.

Without looking at him, she resumed her search. "I guess pretty is too mild. You have a right to expect more powerful descriptions."

He gave her engrossed profile a sideways glance. "If I expect anything, it certainly isn't that."

She slammed another file shut. "Why not? You have the market of *halawah* cornered after all."

Halawah, literally sweetness, was used in Zohayd to describe beauty. That had him turning fully toward her. "Where *do* you come up with these things that you say?"

She flicked him a fleeting glance, closed another file on a sigh of frustration. "That's what women in Zohayd used to say about you. Wonder what they'd say now that your *halawah* is so exacerbated by age it could induce diabetes."

That had a laugh barking from his depths. "Why, thanks. Being called a diabetes risk is certainly a new spin on my supposed good looks."

She tsked. "You know damn well how beautiful you are."

He shook his bemused head at what kept spilling from those dainty lips, compliments with the razor-sharp edges of insults. "No one has accused me of being beautiful before."

"Probably because everyone is programmed to call men handsome or hunks or at most gorgeous. Well, sorry, buddy. You leave all those adjectives in the dust. You're all-out beautiful. It's really quite disgusting."

"Disgusting!"

"Sickeningly so. The resources you must devote to maximizing your assets and maintaining them at this…level…" She tossed him a gesture that eloquently encompassed him from head to toe. "When your looks aren't your livelihood, this is an excess that should be punishable by law."

An incredulous huff escaped him. "It's surreal to hear you say that when my closest people keep telling me the very opposite—that I'm totally neglecting myself."

She slanted him a caustic look. "You have people who can bear being close to you? My deepest condolences to them."

He smiled as if she'd just lavished the most extravagant praise on him. "I'll make sure to relay your sympathies."

Another withering glance came his way before she resumed her work. "I'll give mine directly to Johara. No wonder she's seemed burdened of late. It must be quite a hardship having you for an only brother in general, not to mention having to see you frequently when she's here."

His gaze lengthened on her averted face. Then suddenly everything jolted into place.

Who Kanza *really* was.

She was the new partner that Johara had been waxing poetic about. Now he replayed the times his sister had raved about the woman who'd taken Johara's design house from moderate success to household-name status, this financial marketing guru who had never actually been mentioned by name. But he had no doubt now it was Kanza.

Had Johara never brought up her name because she didn't want to alert him to her intentions, making him resistant to meeting Kanza and predisposed to finding fault with her if he did? If so, then Johara understood him better than Shaheen did, who'd hit him over the head with his intentions and Kanza's name. That *had* backfired. Evidently Johara had reeled Shaheen in, telling her husband not to bring up the subject again and that she'd handle everything from that point on, discreetly. And she had.

Another certainty slotted into place. Johara had kept her business partner in the dark about all this for the same reason.

Which meant that Kanza had no clue this meeting wasn't a coincidence.

The urge to divulge everything about their situation surged from zero to one hundred. He couldn't wait to see the look on her face as the truth of Johara and Shaheen's machinations sank in and to just stand back and enjoy the fireworks.

He turned to her, the words almost on his lips, when another thought hit him.

What if, once he told her, she became stilted, self-conscious? Or worse, *nice?* He couldn't bear the idea that after their invigorating duel of wits, her revitalizing lambasting, she'd suddenly start to sugarcoat her true nature in an attempt to endear herself to him as a potential bride. But worst of all, what if she shut him out completely?

From what he'd found out about her character so far, he'd go with scenario number three as the far more plausible one.

Whichever way this played out, he couldn't risk spoiling her spontaneity or ending this stimulating interlude.

Deciding to keep this juicy tidbit to himself, he said, "Apart from burdening Johara with my existence, I was actually serious for a change. Everyone I meet tells me I've never looked worse. The mirror confirms their opinion."

"I've smacked people upside the head for less, buddy." She narrowed her eyes at him, as if charting the trajectory of the smack he'd earn if he weren't careful. "Nothing annoys me more than false modesty, so if you don't want me to muss that perfectly styled mane of yours, watch it."

Suddenly it was important for him to settle this with her. "There is no trace of anything false in what I'm saying—modesty or otherwise. I really have been in bad shape and have been getting progressively worse for over a year now."

This gave her pause for a moment, something like contrition or sympathy coming into her eyes.

Before he could be sure, it was gone, her fathomless eyes glittering with annoyance again. "You mean you've looked better than this? Any better and you should be...arrested or something."

Something warm seeped through his bones, brought that unfamiliar smile to his lips again. "Though I barely give the way I look any thought, you managed what I thought impossible. You flattered me in a way I never was before."

She grimaced as if at some terrible taste. "Hello? Wasn't I speaking English just now? Flattering you isn't among the things I would ever do, even at gunpoint."

"Sorry if this causes you an allergic reaction, but that is exactly what you did, when I've been looking at myself lately and finding only a depleted wretch looking back at me."

She opened her mouth to deliver another disparaging blow, before she closed it, her eyes narrowing contemplatively over his face.

"Now I'm looking for it. I guess, yeah, I see it. But it sort of...roughens your slickness and gives you a simulation of humanity that makes you look better than your former overly polished perfection. Figures, huh? Instead of looking like crap, you manage to make wretched and depleted work for you."

He abandoned any pretense of looking through the files and turned to her, arms folded over his chest. "Okay. I get it. You despise the hell out of me. Are you going to tell me what I ever did to deserve your wrath, Kanza?"

When she heard her name on his lips, something blipped in her eyes. It was gone again before he could latch on to it, and she reverted back to full-blast disdain mode. "Give the poor, depleted Pirate an energy bar. He's exerted himself digging through his hard drive's trash and recognized me. And even after he did, he still asks. What? You think your transgressions should have been dropped from the record by time?"

"Which transgressions are we talking about here?"

"Yeah, with multitudes to pick from, you can't even figure out which ones I'm referring to."

"Though I'm finding your bashing delightful, even therapeutic, my curiosity levels are edging into the danger zone. How about you put me out of my misery and enlighten me as to what exactly I'm paying the price for now?"

Her lips twisted disbelievingly. "You've really forgotten, haven't you?" At his unrepentant yet impatient nod, she rolled her eyes and turned back to the files, muttering under her breath. "You can go rack your brains with a rake for the answer for all I care. I'm not helping you scratch that itch."

"Since there's no way I've forgotten anything I did to you that could cause such an everlasting grudge..." He paused, frowned then exclaimed, "Don't tell me this is about Maysoon!"

"*And* he remembers. In a way that adds more insult to injury. You're a species of one, aren't you, Aram Nazaryan?"

Before he could say anything, she strode away, clearly not intending to let him pursue the subject. He could push his luck but doubted she'd oblige him.

But at least he now knew where this animosity was coming from. While he hadn't factored in that this would be her stance regarding the fiasco between him and Maysoon, it seemed she had accumulated an unhealthy dose of prejudice against him from the time he'd been briefly engaged to her half sister. And she'd added an impressive amount of further bias ever since.

She slammed another filing cabinet shut. "This damn

file isn't here." She suddenly turned on him. "But you are. What the hell are you doing here, anyway?"

So it had finally sunk in, the improbability of his stumbling in on her here in his sister's office.

Having already decided to throw her off, he said, "I was hoping Johara would be working late."

She frowned. "So you don't know that she and Shaheen are throwing a party tonight?"

"They are?" This had to be his best acting moment ever.

She bought it, as evidenced by her return to mockery. "You forgot that, too? Is anything of any importance to you?"

He approached her again with the same caution he would approach a hostile feline. "Why do you assume it's me who forgot and not them who neglected to invite me?"

"Because I'd never believe either Johara or Shaheen would neglect anyone, even you."

When he was a few feet away, he looked down at her, amusement again rising unbidden. "But it's fully believable that I got their invitation and tossed it in the bin unread?"

She shrugged. "Sure. Why not? I'd believe you got a dozen phone calls, too, or even face-to-face invitations and just disregarded them."

"Then I come here to visit my sister because I'm disregarding her?"

"Maybe you need something from her and came to ask for it, even though you won't consider going to her party."

He let out a short, delighted laugh. "You'll go the extra light-year to think the worst of me, won't you?"

"Don't give me any credit. It's you who makes it exceptionally easy to malign you."

Hardly believing how much he was enjoying her onslaught, he shook his head. "One would think Maysoon is your favorite sister and bosom buddy from the way you're hacking at me."

The intensity of her contempt grew hotter. "I would have

hacked at you if you'd done the same to a stranger or even an enemy."

"So your moral code is unaffected by personal considerations. Commendable. But what *have* I done exactly, in your opinion?"

Her snort was so cute, so incongruous, that it had his unfettered laugh ringing out again.

"Oh, you're good. With three words you've turned this from a matter of fact to a matter of opinion. Play another one."

"I'm trying hard to."

"Then *el'ab be'eed.*"

This meant *play far away.* From her, of course.

Something he had no intention of doing. "Won't you at least recite my charges and read me my rights?"

She produced her cell phone. "Nope. I bypassed all that and long pronounced your sentence."

"Shouldn't I be getting parole after ten years?"

"Not when I gave you life in the first place, no."

His whole face was aching. He hadn't smiled this much in…ever. "You're a mean little thing, aren't you?"

"And you're a sleazy huge thing, aren't you?"

He guffawed this time.

Wondering how the hell this pixie was doing this, triggering his humor with every acerbic remark, he headed back to Johara's desk. "So are we done with your search mission? Or going by the aftermath of your efforts, search-and-destroy operation?"

"Just for that," she said as she placed a call, "you put everything back where it belongs."

"I don't think even Johara herself can accomplish that impossibility after the chaos you've wrought."

She flicked him one last annihilating look, then dismissed him as she started speaking into the phone without preamble. "Okay, Jo, I can't find anything that might be the file you described, and I've gone through every shred of paper you got here."

"You mean *we* did." Aram raised his voice to make sure Johara heard him.

An obsidian bolt hit him right between the eyes, had his heart skipping a beat.

He grinned even more widely at her. He had no doubt Johara *had* heard him, but it was clear she'd pretended she hadn't, since Kanza's wrath would have only increased if Johara had made any comment or asked who was with her.

And he'd thought he'd known everything there was to know about his kid sister. Turned out she wasn't only capable of the subterfuge of setting him and her partner up, but of acting seamlessly on the fly, too.

Kanza was frowning now. "What do you mean it's okay? It's not okay. You need the file, and if it's here, I'll find it. Just give me a better description. I might have looked at it a dozen times and didn't recognize it for what it was."

Kanza fell silent for a few moments as Johara answered. He had a feeling she was telling Kanza a load of ultra-convincing bull. By now, he was 100 percent certain that file didn't even exist.

Kanza ended the conversation and confirmed his deductions. "I can't believe it! Johara is now not even sure the file is here at all. Blames it on pregnancy hormones."

Hoping his placating act was half as good as Johara's misleading one, he said, "We only lost an hour of turning her office upside down. Apart from the mess, no harm done."

"First, there's no *we* in the matter. Second, I was here an hour before you breezed in. Third, you *did* breeze in. Can't think of more harm than that. But the good news is I now get to breeze out of here and put an end to this unwelcome and torturous exchange with you."

"Aren't you even going to try to ameliorate the destruction you've left in your wake?"

"Johara insisted I leave everything and just rush over to the party."

So she was invited. Of course. Though from the way she was dressed, no one would think she had anything more glamorous planned than going to the grocery store.

But it was evident she intended to go. That must have been Johara and Shaheen's plan A. They'd invited him to set him and Kanza up at the soirée. And when he'd refused, Johara had improvised find-the-nonexistent-file plan B.

Kanza grabbed a red jacket from one of the couches, which he hadn't noticed before, and shrugged it on before hooking what looked like a small laptop bag across her body.

Then, without even a backward glance at him, she was striding toward the door.

He didn't know how he'd managed to move that fast, but he found himself blocking her path.

This surprised her so much that she bumped into him. He caught an unguarded expression in those bottomless black eyes as she stumbled back. A look of pure vulnerability. As though the steely persona she'd been projecting wasn't the real her, or not the only side to her. As though his nearness unsettled her so much it left her floundering.

A moment later he wondered if he'd imagined what he'd seen, since the look was now gone and annoyance was the only thing left in its place.

He tried what he hoped was the smooth charm he'd seen others practice but had never attempted himself. "How about we breeze out of here together and I drive you to the party?"

"You assume I came here…how? On foot?"

"A pixie like you might have just blinked in here."

"Then I can blink out the same way."

"I'm still offering to conserve your mystic energies."

"Acting the gentleman doesn't become you, and any attempt at simulating one is wasted on me since I'm hardly a damsel in distress. And if you're offering in order to score points with Johara, forget it."

"There you go again—assigning such convoluted motives to my actions when I'm far simpler than you think. I've decided to go to the party, and since you're going, too, you can save your pixie magic, as I have a perfectly mundane car parked in the garage."

"What a coincidence. So do I. Though mine is mundane for real. While yours verges on the supernatural. I hear it talks, thinks, takes your orders, parks itself and knows when to brake and where to go. All it has left to do is make you a sandwich and a cappuccino to become truly sentient."

"I'll see about developing those sandwich- and cappuccino-making capabilities. Thanks for the suggestion. But wouldn't you like to take a spin in my near-sentient car?"

"No. Just like I wouldn't want to be in your near-sentient presence. Now *ann eznak*...or better still, *men ghair eznak*." Then she turned and strode away.

He waited until she exited the room before moving. In moments, his far-longer strides overtook her at the elevators.

Kanza didn't give any indication that she noticed him, going through messages on her phone. She still made no reaction when he boarded the elevator with her and then when he followed her to the garage.

It was only when he tailed her to her car that she finally turned on him. *"What?"*

He gave her his best pseudoinnocent smile and lobbed back her parting shot. "By your leave, or better still without it, I'm escorting you to your car."

She looked him up and down in silence, then turned and took the last strides to a Ford Escape that was the exact color of her jacket. Seemed she was fond of red.

In moments, she drove away with a screech right out of a car chase, which had him jumping out of the way.

He stood watching her taillights flashing as she hit the

brakes at the garage's exit. Grinning to himself, he felt a rush of pure adrenaline flood his system.

She'd really done it. Something no other woman—no other person—had ever done.

She'd turned him down.

No…it was more that that. She'd *rebuffed* him.

Well. There was only one thing he could do now.

Give chase.

Three

Kanza resisted the urge to floor the gas pedal.

That…rat was following her.

That colossal, cruelly magnificent rat.

Though the way he made her feel was that *she* was the rat, running for her life, growing more frantic by the breath, chased by a majestic, terminally bored cat who'd gotten it in his mind to chase her…just for the hell of it.

She snatched another look in the rearview mirror.

Yep. There he still was. Driving safely, damn him, keeping the length of three cars between them, almost to the inch. He'd probably told his pet car how far away it should stick to her car's butt. The constant distance was more nerve-racking than if he'd kept approaching and receding, if he'd made any indication that he was expending any effort in keeping up with her.

She knew he didn't really want to catch her. He was just exercising the prerogative of his havoc-inducing powers. He was doing this to rattle her. To show her that no one refused him, that he'd do whatever he pleased, even if it infringed on others. Preferably if it did.

It made her want to slam the brakes in the middle of the

road, force him to stop right behind her. Then she'd get down, walk over there and haul him out of his car and… and… What?

Bite mouthfuls out of his gorgeous bod? Swipe his keys and cell phone and leave him stranded on the side of the road?

Evidently, from the maddening time she'd just spent in his company, he'd probably enjoy the hell out of whatever she did. She *had* tried her level worst back in Johara's office, and that insensitive lout had seemed to be having a ball, thinking every insult out of her mouth was a hoot. Seemed his jaded blood levels had long been toxic and now any form of abuse was a stimulant.

Gritting her teeth all the way to Johara and Shaheen's place, she kept taking compulsive glances back at this incorrigible predator who tailed her in such unhurried pursuit.

Twenty minutes later, she parked the car in the garage, filled her lungs with air. Then, holding it as if she was bracing for a blow, she got out.

Out of the corner of her eye she could estimate he'd parked, too. Three empty car places away. He was really going the distance to maintain the joke, wasn't he?

Fine. Let him have his fun. Which would only be exacerbated if she made any response. She wouldn't.

When she was at the elevator, she stopped, a groan escaping her. Aram had frazzled her so much that she'd left Johara and Shaheen's housewarming present, along with the Arabian horse miniature set she'd promised Gharam, in the trunk.

Cursing him to grow a billion blue blistering barnacles, she turned on her heel and stalked back to the car. She passed him on her way back, as he'd been following in her wake, maintaining the equivalent of three paces behind her.

Feeling his gaze on her like the heaviest embarrassment she'd ever suffered, she retrieved the boxes. Just as the tailgate clicked closed, she almost knocked her head against it in chagrin. She'd forgotten to change her sneakers.

Great. This guy was frying her synapses even at fifty paces, where he was standing serenely by the elevator, awaiting her return. Maybe she should just forget about changing the sneakers. Or better still, hurl them at him.

But it was one thing to skip around in those sneakers, another to attend Johara and Shaheen's chic party in them. It was bad enough she'd be the most underdressed one around, as usual.

Forcing herself to breathe calmly, she reopened the tailgate and hopped on the edge of the trunk. He'd just have to bear the excitement of watching her change into slightly less nondescript two-inch heels. At least those were black and didn't clash like a chalk aberration on a black background.

In two minutes she was back at the elevators, hoisting the boxes—each under an arm. Contrary to her expectations, he didn't offer to help her carry them. Then he didn't even board the elevator with her. Instead, he just stood there in that disconcerting calm while the doors closed. Though she was again pretending to be busy with her phone, she knew he didn't pry his gaze from her face. And that he had that infuriating smile on his all the time.

Sensing she'd gotten only a short-lived respite since he was certain to follow her up at his own pace, she knew her smile was on the verge of shattering as Johara received her at the door. It must have been her own tension that made her imagine that Johara looked disappointed. For why would she be, when she'd already known she hadn't found her file and had been the one to insist Kanza stop searching for it?

Speculation evaporated as Johara exclaimed over Kanza's gifts and ushered her toward Shaheen and Gharam. But barely three minutes later, Johara excused herself and hurried to the door again.

Though Kanza was certain it was *him,* her breath still

caught in her throat, and her heart sputtered like a malfunctioning throttle.

Ya Ullah... Why was she letting this virtuoso manipulator pull her strings like this?

The surge of fury manifested in exaggerated gaiety with Shaheen and Gharam. But a minute later Shaheen excused himself, too, and rushed away with Gharam to join his wife in welcoming his so-called best friend. She almost blurted out that Aram was here only to annoy her, not to see him or his sister, and that Shaheen should do himself a favor and find himself a new best friend, since *that* one cared about no one but himself.

Biting her tongue and striding deeper into the penthouse, she forced herself to mingle, which usually rated right with anesthesia-free tooth extractions on her list of favorite pastimes. However, right now, it felt like the most desirable thing ever, compared to being exposed to Aram Nazaryan again.

But to her surprise, she wasn't.

After an hour passed, throughout which she'd felt his eyes constantly on her, he'd made no attempt to approach her, and her tension started to dissipate.

It seemed her novelty to him had worn off. He must be wondering why the hell he'd taken his challenge this far—at the price of suffering the company of actual human beings. Ones who clearly loved him, though why, she'd never understand.

She still welcomed the distraction when Johara asked her to put the horse set in their family living room away from Gharam's determined-to-take-them-apart hands. The two-and-a-half-year-old tyke was one unstoppable girl who everyone said took after her maternal uncle. Clearly, in nature as well as looks.

She'd finished her chore and was debating what was more moronic—that she was this affected by Aram's presence or that her relief at the end of this perplexing interlude was mixed with what infuriatingly resembled letdown—when it felt as if a thousand volts of electricity zapped her. His dark, velvety baritone that drenched her every receptor in paralysis.

It was long, heart-thudding moments before what he'd said made sense.

"I'm petitioning for a reopening of my case."

She didn't turn to him. She couldn't.

For the second time tonight, he'd snuck up on her, startling the reins of volition out of her reach.

But this time, courtesy of the building tension that had been defused in false security, the surprise incapacitated her.

When she didn't turn, it was Aram who circled her in a wide arc, coming to face her at that distance he'd been maintaining, as if he was a hunter who knew he had his quarry cornered yet still wasn't taking any chances he'd get a set of claws across the face.

And as usual with him around, she felt the spacious, ingeniously decorated room shrink and fade away, her senses converging like a spotlight on him.

It was always a shock to the system beholding him. He was without any doubt the most beautiful creature she'd ever seen. Damn him.

She'd bet it was beyond anyone alive not to be awed by his sheer grandeur and presence, to not gape as they drank in the details of what made him what he was. She remembered with acute vividness the first time she'd seen him. She *had* gaped then and every time she'd seen him afterward, trying to wrap her mind around how anyone could be endowed with so much magnificence.

He lived up to his pseudonym—a pirate from a fairy tale, imposing, imperious, mysterious with a dark, ruthless edge to his beauty, making him…utterly compelling.

It still seemed unbelievable that he was Johara's brother. Apart from both of them possessing a level of beauty that was spellbinding, verging on painful to behold, they looked nothing alike. While Johara had the most amazing golden hair, molten chocolate eyes and thick cream complexion, Aram was her total opposite. But after she'd seen both their parents, she'd realized he'd manifested the absolute best in both, too.

His eyes were a more dazzling shade of azure than that of his French mother's—the most vivid, hypnotic color she'd ever seen. From his mother, too, and her family, he'd also inherited his prodigious height and amplified it. He'd added a generous brush of burnished copper to his Armenian-American father's swarthy complexion, a deepened gloss and luxury to his raven mane and an enhanced bulk and breadth to his physique.

Then came the details. And the devil was very much in those. A dancing, laughing, knowing one, aware of the exact measure of their unstoppable influence. Of every slash and hollow and plane of a face stamped with splendor and uniqueness, every bulge and sweep and slope of a body emanating maleness and strength, every move and glance and intonation demonstrating grace and manliness, power and perfection. All in all, he was glory personified.

Now, exuding enough charisma and confidence to power a small city, he towered across from her, calmly sweeping his silk black jacket out of the way, shoving his hands into his pockets. The movement had the cream shirt stretching over the expanse of virility it clung to. Her lips tingled as his chiseled mouth quirked up into that lethal smile.

"I submit a motion that I have been unjustly tried."

Aram's obvious enjoyment, not to mention his biding his time before springing his presence on her again, made retaliation a necessity.

Her voice, when she managed to operate her vocal cords, thankfully sounded cool and dismissive. "And I submit you've not only gotten away with your crimes but you've been phenomenally rewarded for them."

"If you're referring to my current business success, how are you managing to correlate it to my alleged crimes?"

She fought not to lick the dryness from her lips, to bite into the numbness that was spreading through them. "I'm managing because you've built said success using the same principles with which you perpetrated those crimes."

His eyes literally glittered with mischief, becoming bluer before her dazzled ones. "Then I am submitting that those principles you ascribe to me and your proof of them were built around pure circumstantial evidence."

Her eyebrows shot up. "So you're not after a retrial. What you really want is your whole criminal record expunged."

He raised those large, perfectly formed hands like someone blocking blows. "I wouldn't dream of universally dismissing my convictions." His painstakingly sculpted lips curled into a delicious grin. "That would be pushing my luck. But I do demand an actual primary hearing of my testimony, since I distinctly remember one was never taken."

Although she felt her heart sputtering out of control, she tried to match his composure outwardly. "Who says you get a hearing at all? You certainly didn't grant others such mercy or consideration."

The scorching amusement in those gemlike eyes remained unperturbed. "By others you mean Maysoon, I assume?"

"Hers was the case I observed firsthand. As I am a stickler for justice, I will not pass judgment on those I know of only through secondhand testimonies and hearsay."

His eyes widened on what looked like genuine surprise.

Yeah, right. As if he could feel anything for real.

"That's very…progressive of you. Elevated, even." At her baleful glance, something that simulated seriousness took over his expression. "No, I mean it. In my experience, when people don't like someone, they demonize them wholesale, stop granting them even the possibility of fairness."

She pursed her lips, refusing to consider the possibility of his sincerity. "Lauding my merits won't work, you know."

"In granting me a hearing?"

"In granting you leniency you haven't earned and certainly don't deserve." He opened his mouth, and she raised her hand. "Don't you think you've taken your joke far enough?"

For a moment he looked actually confused before a careful expression replaced uncertainty. "What joke, exactly?"

She rolled her eyes. "Spare me."

"Or you'll spear me?" At her exasperated rumble, he raised his hands again, the coaxing in his eyes rising another notch. "That *was* lame. But I really don't know what you're talking about. I am barely keeping up with you."

"Yeah, right. Since you materialized behind me like some capricious spirit, you've been ready with something right off the smart-ass chart before I've even finished speaking."

He shook his head, causing his collar-length mane to undulate. "If you think that was easy, think again. You're making me struggle for every inch before you snatch it away with your next lob. For the first time in my life I have no idea what will spill out of someone's lips next, so give me a break."

"I would ask where you want it, but I have to be realistic. Considering our respective physiques, I probably can't give you one without the help of heavy, blunt objects."

The next moment, all her nerves fired up as he proceeded to subject her to the sight and sound of his all-out amusement, a demonstration so…virile, so debilitating, each peal was a new bolt forking through her nervous system.

When he at last brought his mirth under control, his lips remained stretched the widest she'd seen them, showing off that set of extraordinary white teeth in the most devastating smile she'd had the misfortune of witnessing. He even wiped away a couple of tears of hilarity. "You can give me compound fractures with your tongue alone. As for your glares, we're talking incineration."

Hating that even when he was out of breath and wheezing, he sounded more hard-hitting for it, she gritted out, "If I could do that, it would be the least I owe you."

"What have I done *now?*" Even his pseudolament was scrumptious. This guy needed some kind of quarantine. He shouldn't be left free to roam the realm of flimsy mortals. "Is this about the joke you've accused me of perpetrating?"

"There's no accusation here—just statement of fact. You've been enjoying one big fat joke at my expense since you stumbled on me in Johara's office."

His eyes sobered at once, filling with something even more distressing than mischief and humor. Indulgence? "I've been relishing the experience immensely, but not as a joke and certainly not at your expense."

Her heart gave her ribs another vicious kick. She had to stop this before her heart literally bruised.

She raised her hands. "Okay, this is going nowhere. Let's say I believe you. Give me another reason you're doing this. And don't tell me that you care one way or the other what I think in general or what I think of you specifically. You don't care about what anyone thinks."

The earnestness in his eyes deepened. "You're right. I care nothing for what others think of me."

"And you're absolutely right not to."

That seemed to stun him yet again. "I am?" At her nod, he prodded, "That includes *everyone?*"

She nodded again. "Of course. What other people think of you, no matter who they are, is irrelevant. Unsolicited opinions are usually a hindrance and a source of discontentment, if not outright unhappiness. So carry on not caring, go take your leave from Johara and Shaheen and return to your universe where no one's opinion matters…as it shouldn't."

"At least grant me the right to care or not care." Those unbelievable eyes seemed to penetrate right through her as his gaze narrowed in on her. "And whether it comes under caring or not, I do happen to be extremely interested in your opinion of me. Now, let me escort you back to the party. Let me get us a drink over which we'll reopen my case and explore the possibility of adjusting your opinion of me—at least to a degree."

She arched a brow. "You mean you'd settle for adjusting my opinion of you from horrific to just plain horrid?"

"Who knows, maybe while retrying my case, your unwavering sense of justice will lead you to adjusting it to plain misjudged."

"Or maybe just downright wretched."

He hit her with another of his pouts. Then he raised the level of chaos and laughed again, his merriment as potent as everything else about him. "I'd take that."

Trying to convince her heart to slot back into its usual place after its latest somersault, she again tried her best glower. It had no effect on him, as usual. Worse. It had the opposite effect to what she'd perfected it for. He looked at her as if her glare was the cutest thing he'd seen.

She voiced her frustration. "You talk about my incinerating glares, but I could be throwing cotton balls or rose petals at you for all the effect they have on you."

"It's not your glares that are ineffective. It's me who's discovering a penchant for incineration."

Instead of appeasing her, it annoyed her more. "I'll have you know I've reduced other men to dust with those scowls. No one has withstood a minute in my presence once I engaged annihilate mode." She lifted her chin. "But you seem to need specifically designed weapons. If I go along with you in this game you got it in your mind to play, it'll be so I can find out if you have an Achilles' heel."

"I have no idea if I have that." His gaze grew thoughtful. "Would you use it to…annihilate me if you discovered it?"

She gave him one of her patented sizing-up glances and regretted it midway. She must quit trying her usual strategies with him. Not only because they always backfired, but it wasn't advisable to expose herself to another distressing dose of his wonders.

She returned to his eyes, those turquoise depths that exuded the ferocity of his intellect and the power of his wit, and found gazing into them just as taxing to her circulatory system.

She sighed, more vexed with her own inability to moderate her reactions than with him. "Nah. I'll just be satisfied knowing your Achilles' heel exists and you're not invulnerable. And maybe, if you get too obnoxious, I'll use my knowledge as leverage to make you back off."

That current of mischief and challenge in his eyes spiked. "It goes against my nature to back off."

"Not even under threat of…annihilation?"

"Especially then. I'd probably beg you to use whatever fatal weakness you discover just to find out how it feels."

"Wow. You're jaded to the point of numbness, aren't you?"

"You've got me figured out, don't you? Or do you? Shall we find out?"

It was clear this monolith would stand there and spar with her until she agreed to this "retrial" of his. If she was in her own domain or on neutral ground, or at least somewhere without a hundred witnesses blocking her only escape route, she would have slammed him with something cutting and walked out as she'd done in Johara's office.

But she couldn't inflict on her friends the scene this gorgeous jerk would instigate if he didn't have his way. She bet he knew she suffered from those scruples, was using the knowledge to corner her into participating in his game.

"You're counting on my inability to risk spoiling Johara and Shaheen's party, aren't you?"

His blink was all innocence, and downright evil for it. "I thought you didn't care what other people thought."

"I don't, not when it comes to how I choose to live my

life. But I do care about what others think of my actions that directly impact them. And if I walk out now, you'll tail me in the most obvious, disruptive way you can, generating curiosity and speculation, which would end up putting a damper on Johara and Shaheen's party." Her eyes narrowed as another thought hit her. "Now I am wondering if maybe they *didn't* extend an invitation to you after all because they've been burned by your sabotage before."

He pounced on that, took it where she couldn't have anticipated. "So you're considering changing your mind about whether I was invited? See? Maybe you'll change your mind about everything else if you give me a chance."

She blew out a breath in exasperation. "I only change my mind for the worse…or worst."

"You're one tiny bundle of nastiness, aren't you?" His smile said he thought that the best thing to aspire to be.

She tossed her head, infusing her disadvantaged stature with all the belittling she could muster. "Again with the size references."

"It was you who started using mine in derogatory terms. Then you moved on to my looks, then my character, then my history, and if there were more components to me, I bet you'd have pummeled through them, too."

Refusing to rise to the bait, she turned around and stomped away.

He followed her. Keeping those famous three steps behind. With his footfalls being soundless, she could pinpoint his location only by the chuckles rumbling in the depths of his massive chest. When those ended, his overpowering presence took over, cocooning her all the way to the expansive reception area.

Absorbed in warding off his influence, she could barely register the ultraelegant surroundings or the dozens of chic people milling around. No one noticed her, as usual, but everyone's gaze was drawn to the nonchalant predator behind her. Abhorring the thought of having everyone's eyes on her by association once they realized he was following her, she continued walking where she hoped the least amount of spectators were around.

She stepped out onto the wraparound terrace that overlooked the now-shrouded-in-darkness Central Park, with Manhattan glittering like fiery jewels beyond its extensive domain. Stopping at the three-foot-high brushed stainless steel and Plexiglas railings, gazing out into the moonlit night, she shivered as September's high-altitude wind hit her overheating body. But she preferred hypothermia to the burning speculation that being in Aram Nazaryan's company would have provoked. Not that she'd managed to escape that totally. The few people who'd had the same idea of seeking privacy out here did their part in singeing her with their curiosity.

She hugged herself to ward off the discomfort of their interest more than the sting of the wind. He made it worse, drenching her in the dark spell of his voice.

"Can I offer you my jacket, or would I have my head bitten off again?"

Barely controlling a shudder, she pretended she was flipping her hair away. "Your head is still on your shoulders. Don't push your luck if you want to keep it there."

His lips pursed in contemplation as he watched her suppress another shudder. "You're one of those independent pains who'd freeze to death before letting people pay them courtesies, aren't you?"

"You're one of those imposing pains who force people into the cold, then inflict their jackets on them and call their imposition courtesy, aren't you?"

"I would have settled for remaining inside where it's toasty. You're the one who led me out here to freeze."

"If you're freezing, don't go playing Superman and volunteering your jacket."

That ever-hovering smile caught fire again. "How about we both mosey on round the corner? Since you're the one who decided to hold my retrial thirty floors up and in the open, I at least motion to do it away from the draft."

"You're also one of those gigantic pains who love to marvel at the sound of their own cleverness, aren't you?" She tossed the words back as she walked ahead to do as he'd suggested.

His answer felt like a wave of heat carrying on the whistling wind. "Just observing a meteorological fact."

As he'd projected, the moment they turned the corner, the wind died down, leaving only comfortable coolness to contend with.

She turned to him at the railings. "Stop right there." He halted at once, perplexity entering his gaze. "You're in the perfect position to shield me from any draft. A good use at last for this superfluous breadth and bulk of yours."

Amusement flooded back into his eyes, radiated hypnotic azure in the moonlight. "So you're only averse to voluntary courtesy on my part, but using me as an unintentional barrier is okay with you."

"Perfectly so. I don't intend to suffer from hypothermia because of the situation you imposed on me."

"I made you come out here?"

"Yes, you did."

"And how did I do that?"

"You made escaping the curiosity, not to mention the jealousy, of all present a necessity."

"Jealousy!" His eyebrows disappeared into the layers of satin hair the wind had flopped over his forehead.

"Every person in there, man or woman, would give anything to be in my place, having your private audience." She gave an exaggerated sigh. "If only they knew I'd donate the *privilege* if I could with a sizable check on top as bonus."

His chuckle revved inside his chest again and in her bones. "That *privilege* is nontransferable. You're stuck with it. So before we convene, what shall I get you?"

"Why shouldn't I be the one to get you something?"

His nod was all concession. "Why shouldn't you, indeed?"

She nodded, too, slowly, totally unable to predict him and feeling more out of her depth by the second for it. "Be specific about what you prefer. I hate guessing."

"I'm flabbergasted you're actually considering my preferences. But I'll go with anything nonalcoholic. I'm driving." Considering he'd placed his order, she started to turn around and he stopped her. "And, Kanza...can you possibly also make it something nonpoisoned and curse free?"

Muttering "smart-ass" and zapping him with her harshest parting glance, which only dissipated against his force field and was received by another chuckle, she strode away.

On reentering the reception, she groaned out loud as she immediately felt the weight of Johara's gaze zooming in on her. She'd no doubt noticed Aram marching behind her across the penthouse and must be bursting with curiosity about how they'd met and why that older brother of hers had gotten it into his mind to follow her around.

Johara just had to bear not knowing. She couldn't worry about her now. One Nazaryan at a time.

She grabbed a glass of cranberry-apple juice from a passing waiter and strode back to the terrace, this time exiting from where she'd left Aram. As soon as she did, she nearly tripped, as her heartbeat did.

Aram was at the railing, two dozen paces away with his back to her. He was silhouetted against the rising moon, hands gripping the bar, looking like a modern statue of a Titan. The only animate things about him were the satin stirring around his majestic head in the tranquil breeze and the silk rustling around his steel-fleshed frame.

But apart from his physical glory, there was something about his pose as he stared out into the night—in the slight slump of his Herculean shoulders, dimming that indomitable vibe—that disturbed her. Whatever it was, it forced her to reconsider her disbelief of his assertion that he'd never felt worse. Made her feel guilty about how she'd been bashing him, believing him invincible.

Then he turned around, as if he'd felt her presence, and his eyes lit up again with that potent merriment and mischief, and all empathy evaporated in a wave of instinctive challenge and chagrined response.

How was it even possible? That after all these years he remained the one man who managed to wring an explosive mixture of fascination and detestation from her?

From the first time she'd laid eyes on him when she'd been seventeen, she'd thought him the most magnificent male in existence, one who compounded his overwhelming physical assets with an array of even more impressive superiorities. He'd been the only one who could breach her composure and tongue-tie her just by walking into a room. That had only earned him a harder crash from the pedestal she'd placed him on, when he'd proved to be just another predictable male, one who considered only a woman's looks and status no matter her character. Why else would he have gotten involved with her spoiled and vapid half sister? Her opinion of him would have been salvaged when he'd walked away from Maysoon, if—and it was an insurmountable if— he hadn't been needlessly, shockingly cruel in doing so.

Remembered outrage rose as she stopped before him and foisted the drink into his hand. It rose higher when she couldn't help watching how his fingers closed around the glass, the grace, power and economy of the movement. It made her want to whack herself and him upside the head.

She had to get this ridiculous interlude over with.

"Without further ado, let's get on with your preposterous retrial."

That gargantuan swine gave a superb pretense of wiping levity from his face, replacing it with earnestness.

"It's going to be the fastest one in history. Your indictment was unequivocal and the evidence against you overwhelming. Whatever her faults, Maysoon loved you, and you kicked her out of your life. Then when she was down, you kicked her again—almost literally and very publicly. You left her in a heap on the ground and walked away unscathed, and then went on to prosper beyond any expectations. While she went on to waste her life, almost self-destruct in one failed relationship after another. If I'd judged your case then, I would have passed the harshest sentence. In any retrial, I'd still pronounce you guilty and judge that you be subjected to character execution."

Four

Aram stared at the diminutive firebrand who was the first woman who'd ever fetched him a drink, then followed up by sentencing his character to death.

Both action and indictment should have elated the hell out of him, as everything from her tonight had. But the expected exhilaration didn't come; something unsettling spread inside him instead. For what if her opinion of him was too entrenched and he couldn't adjust it?

He transferred his gaze to the burgundy depths in the glass she'd just handed him, collecting his thoughts.

Although he'd been keeping it light and teasing, he knew this had suddenly become serious. He had to be careful what to say from now on. If he messed this up, she'd never let him close enough again to have another round. That would be it.

And he couldn't let that be it. He wasn't even going to entertain that possibility. He might have lost many things in his life, but he wasn't going to lose this.

He raised his eyes to meet hers. It was as if they held pieces of the velvet night in their darkest depths. She was waiting, playing by the rules he'd improvised, giving him a chance to defend himself. He had no doubt it would be his one and only chance. He had to make it work.

He inhaled. "I submit that your so-called overwhelming evidence was all circumstantial and unreliable. I did none of the things you've just accused me of. Cite every shred of evidence you think you have, and I'll debunk each one for you."

Her face tilted up at him, sending that amazing wealth of hair cascading with an audible sigh to one side. "You didn't kick Maysoon out of your life?"

"Not in the way you're painting."

"How would you paint it? In black-and-white? In full color? Or because the memory must have faded—in sepia?"

"Who's being a smart-ass now?" At her nonchalant shrug, he pressed on. "What do you know about what happened between Maysoon and me? Apart from her demonizing accounts and your own no less prejudiced observations?"

"Since my observations were so off base, why don't you tell me your own version?"

Having gotten so used to her contention, he was worried by her acquiescence.

He exhaled to release the rising tension. "I assume you knew what your half sister was like? Maybe the impossible has happened and she's evolved by age, but back then, she was…intolerable."

"But of course you found that out after you became engaged to her."

"No. Before."

As he waited for her censure to surpass its previous levels, her gaze only grew thoughtful.

There was no predicting her, was there?

"And you still went through with it. Why?"

"Because I was stupid." Her eyes widened at his harsh admission. She must have thought he'd come up with some excuse to make his actions seem less pathetic and more defensible. He would have done that with anyone else. But with her, he just wanted to have the whole truth out. "I wanted to get married and have a family, but I had no idea how to go about doing that. I thought I'd never leave Zohayd at the time and I'd have to choose a woman from those available. But there was no one I looked at twice, let alone considered for anything lasting. So when Maysoon started pursuing me…"

"Watch it." Her interjection was almost soft. It stopped him in his tracks harder than if she'd bitten it off. "You'll veer off into the land of fabrication if you use this rationale for choosing Maysoon. Using the pursuit criterion, you should have ended up with a harem, since women of all ages in Zohayd chased after you."

"Now who's taking a stroll in the land of exaggeration? Not all women were after me. Aliyah and Laylah, for instance, considered me only one of the family. And you didn't consider me human at all, I believe, let alone male."

Her eyes glittered with the moon's reflected silver as she ignored his statement concerning her. "And that's what? Two females out of two million?"

"Whatever the number of women who pursued me, they were after me as an adventure, and each soon gave up when I made it clear I wasn't into the kind of…entertainment they were after. I wanted a committed relationship at the time."

"And you're saying that none wanted that? Or that none seemed a better choice than Maysoon for said relationship?"

"Compared to Maysoon's pursuit, they were all slouches. And your sister did look like the best deal. Suitable age, easy on the eyes and very, very determined. Sure, she was volatile and superficial, but when her pursuit didn't wane for a whole year, I thought it meant she *really* liked what she saw."

"Her along with everyone with eyes or a brain wave."

Again she managed to make the compliment the most

abrasive form of condemnation, arousing that stinging pleasure he was getting too used to.

"I'm not talking about my alleged 'beauty' here. I thought
she liked *me,* and that meant a lot then. I knew how I was
viewed in the royal circles in Zohayd, what my attraction
was to the women you cite as my hordes of pursuers. I was
this exotic foreigner of mixed descent from a much lower
social class that they could have a safe and forbidden fling
with. Many thought they could keep me as their boy toy."

Something came into her eyes. Sympathy? Empathy?

It was probably ridicule, and he was imagining things.

"You were hardly a boy," she murmured.

"Their gigolo, then. In any event, I thought Maysoon
viewed me differently. Her pursuit in spite of our class dif-
ferences and the fact that I was hardly an ideal groom for a
princess made me think she was one of those rare women
who appreciated a man for himself. I thought this alone
made up for all her personal shortcomings. And who was
I to consider those when I was riddled with my own?" He
emptied his lungs on a harsh exhalation. "Turned out she
was just attracted to me as a spoiled brat would be to a toy
she fancied and couldn't have. Most likely because some of
the women in her inner circle must have made me a topic
of giggling lust, maybe even challenge, and being patho-
logically competitive herself, she wanted to be the one to
triumph over them."

Kanza's eyes filled with skepticism, but she let it go un-
voiced and allowed him to continue.

"And the moment she did she started trying to strip me
bare to dress me up into the kind of toy she had in mind all
along. She started telling me how I must behave, in private
and public, how I must distance myself from my father,
whom she made clear she considered the hired help." He
drew in a sharp inhalation laden with his still-reverberating
chagrin on his father's account. "And it didn't end there.
She dictated who I should get close to, how I must kiss up

to Shaheen's brothers now that he was gone, play on my former relationship with him to gain a 'respectable' position within the kingdom and wheedle financial help in setting up a business like theirs so I would become as rich as possible."

The cynicism in Kanza's eyes had frozen. There was nothing in them now. A very careful nothing. As if she didn't know how to react to the influx of new information.

He went on. "And she was in a rabid hurry for me to do all that. She couldn't wait to have me pick up the tab of her extravagant existence—which she'd thought so disadvantaged—and informed me that as her husband it would be my duty to raise her up to a whole new level of excess." He scrubbed a hand across his jaw. "In the four months' duration of the engagement, I was so stunned by the depths of her shallowness, so taken aback by the audacity of her demands and the intensity of her tantrums, that I didn't react. Then came the night of that ball."

She'd been there that night. In one of those horrific get-ups and alien makeup. He now remembered vividly that she'd been the last thing he'd seen as he'd walked out, standing there over Maysoon, glaring at him with loathing in her eyes.

There was nothing but absorption in her eyes now. She was evidently waiting to see if his version of that ill-fated night's events would change the opinion she'd long held of him, built on her interpretation of its events.

He felt that his next words would decide if she'd ever let him near again. He had to make them count. The only way he could do that was to be as brutally honest as possible.

"Maysoon dragged me to talk to King Atef and Amjad. But when I didn't take her heavy-handed hints to broach the subject of the high-ranking job she'd heard was open, or the loan she'd been pushing me to ask for, she decided to take control. She extolled my economic theories for Zohayd and made a mess of outlining them. Then she proceeded to massacre my personal business plans, which I'd once made the mistake of trying to explain to her. She became terminally obvious as she bragged how anyone getting on with me on the ground level with a sizable investment would reap *millions*." He huffed a bitter laugh. "For a mercenary soul, she knew nothing about the real value of money, since she'd never made a cent and had never even glanced at her own bills."

There was only corroboration in Kanza's eyes now. Knowing her half sister, she must have known the accuracy of this assessment.

He continued. "Needless to say, King Atef and Amjad were not impressed, and they must have believed I'd put her up to it. I was tempted to tell them the truth right then and there, that I'd finally faced it that I was just a means to an end to subsidize her wasteful life. Instead, I attempted to curtail the damage she'd done as best I could before excusing myself and making my escape. Not that she'd let me walk away."

Wariness invaded her gaze. She must have realized he'd come to the point where he'd finally explain the fireworks that had ended his life in Zohayd and formed her lasting-till-now opinion of him.

He shoved his hands into his pockets. "She stormed after me, shrieking that I was a moron, a failure, that I didn't know a thing about grabbing opportunities and maximizing my connections. She said my potential for 'infiltrating' the higher echelons of the royal family was why she'd considered me in the first place and that if I wanted to be her husband I'd do anything to ingratiate myself to them and provide her with the lifestyle she deserved."

Her wince was unmistakable. As if, even if she knew full well Maysoon was capable of saying those things and harboring those motivations, she was still embarrassed for her, ashamed on her account.

Suddenly he wanted to go no further, didn't want to

cause her any discomfort. But she was waiting for him to go on. Her eyes were now prodding him to go on.

He did. "It was almost comical, but I wasn't laughing. I wasn't even angry or disappointed or anything else. I was just…done. So I told her that I would have done anything for the woman I married if she had married me for me and not as a potential meal ticket. Then I walked away. Maysoon wasn't the first major error in judgment I made in Zohayd, but she was the one I rectified."

He paused for a moment, then made his concluding statement, the one refuting her major accusation. "If your half sister has been wasting her life and self-destructing, it's because that's what she does with her capriciousness and excesses and superfluous approach to life—not because of anything *I* did to her. And she's certainly not spinning out of control on my account, because I never counted to her."

Kanza stared up at Aram for what felt like a solid hour after he'd finished his *testimony*.

She could still feel his every word all over her like the stings of a thousand wasps.

She'd never even imagined or could have guessed about his situation back in Zohayd, how he'd been targeted and propositioned, how he'd felt unvalued and objectified.

And she'd been just as guilty of wronging him. In her own mind, in her own way, she had discriminated against him, too, if in the totally opposite direction to those women he'd described. While they'd reduced him to a sexual plaything in their minds, or a stepping-stone to a material goal, she'd exalted him to the point where she'd been unable to see beyond his limitless potential. She hadn't suspected that his untouchable self-possession could have been a facade, a defense; had believed him confident to the point of arrogance; equated his powerful influence with ruthlessness; and had assumed that he could have no insecurities, needs or vulnerabilities.

But…wait. *Wait.* This story was incomplete. He'd left out a huge part. A vital one.

She heard her voice, low, strained, wavering on a gust of wind that circumvented the shield of his body. "But you ended up doing what she advised you to do. She just didn't reap the benefit of her efforts, since you kicked her out of your life on her ear and soared so high on your own."

"Now what the hell are you talking about?"

She pulled herself to her full five-foot-two-plus-heels height, attempting to shove herself up into his face. "Did you or didn't you seek the Aal Shalaan Brotherhood in providing you with their far-reaching connections and fat financial support on your launch into billionairedom?"

"Is this what she said I did?" His scoff sounded furious for the first time. So this was his inapproachable line, what would rouse the indolent predator—any insinuations maligning the integrity and autonomy of his success. "And why not? I did know that there was no limit to her vindictiveness, that she'd do and say anything to punish me for escaping her talons. What else did she accuse me of? Maybe that I abused her, too?"

Her own outrage receded at the advance of his, which was so palpable she had no doubt it was real. Her answer stuck in her throat.

She no longer wanted to continue this. She hadn't wanted to start it in the first place. But his eyes were blazing into hers, demanding that she let him know the full details of Maysoon's accusations. And she had to tell him.

"She said you…exploited her, then threw her aside when you had enough of her."

His eyes narrowed to azure lasers. "By exploited, she meant…sexually?" She nodded, and he gave a spectacular snort, a drench of cold sarcasm underscoring his affront. "Would you believe that I never slept with her?"

"Last I heard, 'sleeping' with someone wasn't a prerequisite of being intimate."

"All right, I did try to be a gentleman and spare you the R-rated language. But since being euphemistic doesn't work in criminal cases, let me be explicit. I never had sex with her. In *any* form. *She* did instigate a few instances of heavy petting—which I didn't reciprocate and put an end to when she tried to offer me…sexual favors. Bottom line…beyond a few unenthusiastic-on-my-part kisses, I never breached her 'purity.' And I wasn't even holding back. I just never felt the least temptation. And when I started seeing her true colors and realized what she really wanted from me, I even became repulsed."

Every word had spiked her temperature higher. To her ears, her every instinct, each had possessed the unmistakable texture of truth. But sanctioning them as the new basis for her belief, her view of the past and his character was still difficult. Mainly because it went against everything she'd believed for so long, about him, about men in general.

Feeling her head would burst on fire, she mumbled, "You're telling me you could be so totally immune to a woman as beautiful as Maysoon when she was so very willing, too? I never heard that mental aversion ever interfered with a man's…drive. Maybe you are not human after all."

"Then get this news flash. There are men who don't find a beautiful, willing woman irresistible."

"Yes. Those men are called gay. Are you? Did you maybe discover that you were when you failed to respond to Maysoon?"

She knew she was being childish and that there was no way he was gay. But she was floundering.

"I 'failed to respond' to Maysoon because I'm one of those men who recognizes black widows and instinctively recoils from said intimacies out of self-preservation. Feeling you're being set up for long-term use and abuse is far more effective than an ice-cold shower. Of course, in hindsight, the fact that I was not attracted to her from the start should have been the danger bell that sent me running. But as I said, I was stupid, thinking that marriage didn't have to include sexual compatibility as a necessary ingredient, that beggars shouldn't be choosers."

He shook his head on a huff of deep disgust. "Lord, now I know why everyone treated me as if I was a sexual predator. Even knowing what she's capable of, I never dreamed she'd go as far as slandering herself in a conservative kingdom where a woman's 'honor' is her sexual purity, in order to paint me a darker shade of black."

That was the main reason Kanza had been forced to believe her half sister. She hadn't been able to imagine even Maysoon would harm herself this way if it hadn't been true. And once she'd believed her in this regard, everything else had been swallowed and digested without any thought of scrutiny. But now she couldn't even consider *not* believing him. This was the truth.

This meant that everything she'd assumed about him was a lie. Which left her...where?

Nowhere. Nowhere but in the wrong and not too happy about being forced to readjust her view of him.

Which didn't actually amount to anything. Her opinion had never mattered to anyone—especially not to Aram. All this new information would do now was torment her with guilt over the way she'd treated him. She'd always prided herself on her sense of justice, yet she'd somehow allowed prejudice to override her common sense where he'd been concerned.

The other damage would be to have her rekindled fascination with him unopposed by that buffering detestation. Although it wouldn't make any difference to him how she changed her opinion of him, she couldn't even chart the ramifications to herself. There was no way this wouldn't be a bad thing to her. Very bad.

Snapping out of her reverie, she realized he wasn't even done "testifying" yet. "Now I come to my deposition about your other accusation—of enlisting the Aal Shalaan Brotherhood's help in 'soaring so high.'"

She waved him off, not up to hearing more. "Don't bother."

"Oh, I bother. Am bothered. Very much so."

"Well, that's your problem. I've heard enough."

"But I haven't said enough." He frowned as a shudder shook her. "For a hurricane, it seems you're not impervious to fellow weather conditions. Let's get inside, and I'll field all the curiosity and jealousy you dragged us out here to avoid."

She shuddered again—and not with cold. She was on the verge of combusting with mortification. "It's not the cold that's bothering me."

He gave her one of those patient looks that said he'd withstand any amount of resistance and debate…until he got his way. Then he suddenly advanced on her.

Trapped with the terrace railings at her back, she couldn't have moved if she'd wanted to. She was unable to do anything but stand there helplessly watching him as he neared her in that tranquil prowl, shrugging off his jacket. Then, without touching her, he draped her in it. In what it held of his heat, his scent, his…essence.

For paralyzed moments, feeling as if she was completely enveloped in him, she gazed way up into those preternatural eyes, that slight, spellbinding smile, a quake that originated from a fault line at her very core threatening to break out and engulf her whole.

Before it did, he stepped away, resumed the position she'd told him to maintain as her windshield.

"Now that you're warm, I don't have to feel guilty about rambling on. To explain what happened, I have to outline what happened after that showdown at the ball. I basically found myself a pariah in Zohayd, and I very soon was forced to take the decision to leave. I was preparing to when the Aal Shalaan Brotherhood came to me—all but Amjad, of course. They attempted to dissuade me from leaving, assured me they knew me too well to believe Maysoon's accusations, that they'd resolve everything with their family and Zohaydan society at large if I stayed. They did offer to help me set up my business, to be my partners or to finance me until it took off. But I declined their offer."

She again tried to interject with her insistence that she didn't need him to explain. She believed that had been another of Maysoon's lies. "Aram, I—"

He held up a hand. "Don't take my word for it. Go ask them. I wanted no handouts, but even more, I wanted nothing to maintain any ties to Zohayd after I decided to sever them all forever. I'd remained in Zohayd in the first place for my father, but I felt I hadn't done him any good staying, and after Maysoon's stunt, I knew my presence would cause him nothing but grief." He paused before letting out his breath on a deep sigh. "I had also given up on Shaheen coming back. It was clear that the reconciliation I'd thought being in Zohayd would facilitate wouldn't come to pass."

She heard her voice croaking a question that had long burned in the back of her mind. "Are you going to tell me that Shaheen was to blame for this breakup and alienation, too?"

She hadn't been able to believe the honorable Shaheen could have been responsible for such a rift. Learning of that estrangement after Maysoon's public humiliation *had* entrenched her prejudice against Aram, solidifying her view of him as a callous monster who cast the people who cared for him aside.

Though said view had undergone a marked recalibration, she hoped he'd blame Shaheen as he'd blamed Maysoon. This would put him back in the comfortable dark gray zone.

His next words doused that hope.

"No, that was all my doing. But don't expect me to tell you what I did that was so bad that he fled his own kingdom to get away from me."

"Why not?" she muttered. "Aren't you having a disclosure spree this fine night?"

"You expect me to spill all my secrets all at once?" His feigned horror would have been funny if she was capable of humor now. "Then have nothing more to reveal in future encounters?"

"Did I ask you to tell me *any* secrets? You're the one who's imposing them on me."

His grin was unrepentant. "Let me impose some more on you, then. Just a summation, so grit your teeth and bear it. So…rather than following Maysoon's advice and latching onto Shaheen's brothers for financing, connections and clout, I turned down their generous offers. I had the solid plan, the theoretical knowledge and some practical experience, and I was ready to take the world by storm."

Her sense of fairness reared its head again. "And you certainly did. I am well aware of the global scope of your business management and consultation firm. Many of the major conglomerates I worked with, even whole countries, rely on you to set up, manage and monitor their financial and executive departments. And if you did it all on your own, then you're not as good as they say—you're way better."

Again her testimony seemed to take him by surprise.

His eyes had taken that thoughtful cast again as he said, "Though I'm even more intrigued than ever that you know all that, and I would have liked to take all the credit for the success I've achieved, it didn't happen quite that way. The beginning of my career suffered from some…catastrophic setbacks, to say the least."

"How so?"

Those brilliant eyes darkened with something…vast and too painful. But when he went on, he gave no specifics. "Well, what I thought I knew—my academic degrees, the experience I had in Zohayd—hadn't prepared me for jumping off the deep end with the sharks. But I managed to climb out of the abyss with only a few parts chomped off and launched into my plans with all I had. But I wouldn't have attained my level of success if I hadn't had the phenomenal luck of finding the exact right people to employ. It was together that we 'soared so high.'"

Not taking all the credit for his achievements cast him in an even better light. But there was still one major crime nothing he'd said could exonerate.

"So Maysoon might have been wrong—*was* wrong—about how you made your fortune. But can you blame her for thinking the worst of you? My opening statement in this retrial stands. You didn't have to be so unbelievably cruel in your public humiliation of her."

His stare fixed her for interminable moments, something intense roiling in its depths, something like reluctance, even aversion, as if he hated the response he had to make.

Seeming to reach a difficult decision, he beckoned her nearer.

He thought she'd come closer than that to him? Of her own volition? And why did he even want her to?

When she remained frozen to the spot, he sighed, inched nearer himself. She felt his approach like that of an oncoming train, her every nerve jangling at his increasing proximity.

He stopped a foot away, tilted his head back, exposing his neck to her. She stared at its thick, corded power, her mind stalling. It was as if he was asking her to...to...

"See this?" His purr jolted her out of the waywardness of her thoughts. She blinked at what he was pointing at. Three parallel scars, running from below his right ear halfway down his neck. They'd been hidden beneath his thick, luxurious hair. A current rattled through her at the sight of them. They were clearly very old, and although they weren't hideous, she could tell the injury *had* been. It was because his skin was that perfect, resilient type that healed with minimum scarring that they'd faded to that extent.

He exhaled heavily. "I ended my deposition at the moment I walked away, thought it enough, that any more was overkill. But seems nothing less than full disclosure will do here." He exhaled again, his eyes leveled on hers, totally serious for the first time. "Maysoon gave me this souvenir. She wouldn't let me go just like that. I barely dodged before she slashed across my face and took one eye out."

Kanza shuddered as the scene played in her mind. She did know how hysterical Maysoon could become. She could see her doing that. And she was left-handed…

"I pushed her off me, rushed to the men's room to stem the bleeding and had to lock the door so she wouldn't barge in and continue her frenzy. I got things under control and cleaned myself up, but she pounced on me as soon as I left the sanctuary of the men's room. I couldn't get the hell out of the palace without crossing the ballroom, and I kept pushing her off me all the way there, but once we got back inside, she started screeching.

"As people gathered, she was crying rivers and saying I cheated on her. I just wanted out—at any cost. So I said, 'Yes, I'm the bad guy, and isn't she lucky she's found out before it was too late?' When I tried to extricate myself, she flung herself on the ground, sobbing hysterically that I'd hit her. I couldn't stand around for the rest of her show, so I turned away and left."

He stopped, drew in a huge breath, let it out on a sigh. "But my deposition wouldn't be complete without saying that I've long realized that I owe her a debt of gratitude for everything she did."

Now, *that* stunned her. "You do?"

He nodded. "If her campaign against me hadn't forced me to leave Zohayd, I would have never pursued my own destiny. My experience with her was the perfect example of *assa an takraho sha'an wa howa khairon lakkom.*"

You may hate something and it is for your best.

He'd said that in perfect Arabic. Hearing his majestic voice rumbling the ancient verse was a shock. Maysoon had spoken only English to him, making her think he hadn't learned the language. But it was clear he had—and perfectly. There wasn't the least trace of accent in his pronunciation. He'd said it like a connoisseur of old poetry would.

He cocked that awesome head at her. "So now that you've heard my full testimony, any adjustment in your opinion of me?"

Floundering, wanting for the floor to split and snatch her below, she choked out, "It—it *is* your word against hers."

"Then I am at a disadvantage, since she is your half sister. Though that should be to her disadvantage, since you're probably intimate with all her faults and are used to taking her testimony about anything with a pound of salt. But if for some reason you're still inclined to believe her, then there is only one way for me to have a fair retrial. I demand that you get to know me as thoroughly as you know her."

"What do you mean, get to know you?" She heard the panic that leaped into her voice.

He was patient indulgence itself. "How do people get to know each other?"

"I don't know. How?"

The same forbearance met her retort. "How did you get to know anyone in your orbit?"

"I was thrown with them by accidents of birth or geography or necessity."

That had his heart-stopping smile dawning again. "I'm tempted to think you've been a confirmed misanthrope since you exited the womb."

"According to my mother, they barely extracted me surgically before I clawed my way out of her. She informed me I spoiled the having-babies gig for her forever."

His eyes told her what he thought of her mother. Yeah, him and everyone in the civilized world.

Then his eyes smiled again. "It's a calamity we don't have video documentation of your entry into the world. That would have been footage for the ages. So—" he rubbed his hands together "—when will our next reconnaissance session be?"

Her heart lodged in her throat again. "There will be no next anything."

"Why? Have you passed your judgment again, and it's still execution?"

"No, I've given you a not-guilty verdict, so you can go gallop in the fields free. Now, *ann eznak...*"

"Or better still, *men ghair ezni,* right?"

"See? You can predict me now. I was only diverting when you couldn't guess what I'd say next, but now that you've progressed to completing my sentences, my entertainment value is clearly depleted. Better to quit while we're ahead."

"I beg to differ. Not that I am or was after 'entertainment.' Will you suggest a time and venue, or will you leave it up to me?"

She could swear flames erupted inside her skull.

"You've had your retrial, and I want to salvage what I can of this party," she growled. "Now get out of my way."

As if she hadn't said anything, his eyes laughed at her as he all but crooned, "So you want me to surprise you?"

"Argh!"

Foisting his jacket at him, she pushed past him, barely resisting the urge to break out into a sprint to escape his nerve-fraying chuckles.

She felt those following her even after she'd rejoined the party, when there was no way she could still hear him.

And he thought she'd expose herself to him again?

Hah.

One cataclysmic brush with Aram Nazaryan might have been survivable. But enduring another exposure?

No way.

After all, she didn't have a death wish.

Five

"I see you've found Kanza."

Aram stopped midstride across the penthouse, groaning out loud.

Shaheen. Not the person he wanted to see right now.

But then, he wanted to see no one but that keg of unpredictability who'd skittered away from him again. Though he was betting she wouldn't let him find her again tonight.

While Shaheen wasn't going anywhere before he rubbed his nose in some choice I-told-you-sos.

Deciding on the best defense, he engaged offensive maneuvers. "*Found* her? Don't you mean you and your coconspirator wife threw us together?"

"*I* did nothing but put my foot in it. It's *your* kid sister who pushed things along. But she only 'threw' you two together. You could have extracted yourself in five minutes if she'd miscalculated. But obviously she didn't. From our estimations, you've spent over five hours in Kanza's company. To say you found her…compatible is putting it mildly."

"*Hold* it right there, buddy." He shook his finger at Shaheen. "You're not even going down that road, you hear? I just *talked* to the…to the… God, I can't even find a name

for her. I can't call her girl or woman or anything that…
run-of-the-mill. I don't know what the hell she is."

"As long as it's not monster or goblin anymore, that's a
huge development."

"No, she's certainly neither of those things." And Kanza
the Monster hadn't even been his name for her. It had been
Maysoon's and her friends'. That alone should have made
him disregard it. He'd adopted it only because he couldn't
find an alternative. And Kanza *had* unsettled the hell out
of him back then. She still did—if in a totally different
way. One he still couldn't figure out. "All night I've been
thinking sprite, brownie, pixie…but none of that really de-
scribes her either."

"The word you're looking for is…treasure."

Aram stared at his friend. *"Treasure?"*

Then he blinked. *Kanz* meant treasure. Kanza was the
feminine form. How had he never focused on her name's
meaning?

Though… "Treasure isn't how I'd describe her, either."

"No?" Shaheen quirked an eyebrow. "Maybe not…yet.
She can't be categorized, anyway."

"You got *that* right. But that's as right as you get. I'm not
about to ask for her hand in marriage, so put a lid on it."

"Your…caution is understandable. You met her—the
grown-up her, anyway—only hours ago. You wouldn't be
thinking of anything beyond the moment yet."

"Not yet, not ever. Can't a man enjoy the company of an
unidentifiable being without any further agenda?"

Knowing amusement rose in Shaheen's eyes. "You tell
me. Can he?"

"*Yes,* he can. And he fully intends to. And he wants you
and your much better half to butt out and stay out of this.
Let *him* have *fun* for a change, and don't try to make this
into anything more than it is. Got it?"

Shaheen nodded. "Got it."

He threw his hands in the air. "Why didn't you argue? Now I know I'm in for some nasty surprise down the road."

Abandoning his pretense of seriousness, Shaheen grinned teasingly. "From where I'm standing, you consider the surprise you got a rather delightful one."

"Too many surprises and one is bound to wipe out all good ones before it. It's basic Surprise Law." Folding his arms across his chest, he shot his friend a warning look. "Keep your royal noses out of this, Shaheen. I'm your senior, and even if you don't think so, I do know what's best for me, so permit me the luxury of running my own personal life."

Shaheen's grin only widened. "I already said I...*we* will. Now chill."

"Chill?" Aram grimaced. "You just managed to give me an anxiety attack. God, but you two are hazards."

Shaheen took him around the shoulder. "We've done our parts as catalysts. Now we'll let the experiment progress without further intervention."

He narrowed his eyes at him. "Even if you think I'm messing it up? You won't be tempted to intervene then?"

Shaheen wiggled one eyebrow. "That worry would motivate you not to mess it up, wouldn't it?"

He tore himself away. "Shaheen!"

Shaheen laughed. "I'm just messing with you. You're on your own. Just don't come crying one day that you are."

"I won't." He tsked. "And quit making this what it isn't. I only want to put my finger on what makes her so... unquantifiable."

Sighing dramatically, Shaheen played along. "I guess it's because she's nothing anyone expects a princess, let alone a professional woman, to be. Before she became Johara's partner, I only heard her being described as mousy, awkward, even gauche."

"*What?* Who the hell were those people talking about?"

"*You* had that Kanza the Monster conviction going, too."

"At least 'monster' recognized the sheer force of her character."

Shaheen shrugged. "I think she's simply nice."

An impressive snort escaped him. "Who're you calling nice? That's the last adjective in the English language to describe her. She's no such vague, lukewarm, *benign* thing."

Shaheen's lips twitched. "After an evening in her company, you seem to have become *the* authority on her. So how would *you* describe her?"

"Didn't you hear me when I said that I don't *know* what she is? All I know is that she's an inapproachable bundle of thorns. An unstoppable force of nature, like a…a… hurricane."

"That's more of a natural disaster."

He almost muttered "smart-ass" in the exact way Kanza had to him. He *was* exasperated with having his enthusiasm interpreted into what Shaheen and Johara wanted it to be. When it was like nothing he'd ever felt. It was as unpredictable as that hurricane in question.

One thing he knew for certain, though. He wasn't trying to define it or to direct it. Or expect anything from it. And he sure as hell wasn't attempting to temper it. Not to curb Shaheen's expectations, not for anything.

"Whatever. It's the one description that suits her."

"That would make her Hurricane Kanza."

With that, Shaheen took him back to Johara, where he endured her teasing, too. And he again made her and her incorrigibly romantic spouse promise that they wouldn't interfere.

Then as he left the party, he thought of the name Shaheen had suggested.

Hurricane Kanza. It described her to a tee.

After he'd compared her effect on Johara's office to one a lifetime ago, she had proceeded to tear through him with the uprooting force of one. All he wanted to do now was hurtle into her path again and let her toss him wherever she would.

But she wouldn't do it of her own accord. She must still be processing the revelations that, given her sense of justice, *must* have changed her opinion of him. But it no doubt remained an awkward situation for her, since her prejudice had been long held, and Maysoon was still her half sister.

Not that he would allow any of that to stand in his way. He fully intended to get exposed to her delightful destruction again and again, no matter what it took.

Now he just had to plan his next exposure to her devastation.

Aram eyed Johara's office door, impatience rising.

Kanza was in a morning meeting with his sister. Once that was over, he planned to…intercept her.

He'd done so every day for the past two weeks. But the sprite had given him the slip each time. He never got in more than a few words with her before she blinked out on him like her fellow pixies did. But what words those had been. Like tastings from gourmet masterpieces that only left him starving for a full meal again.

He'd let her wriggle away as part of his investigation into her components and patterns of behavior. It had pleased the hell out of him that he still found the first inscrutable and the second unforeseeable. But today he wasn't letting that steel butterfly flutter away. She was having a whole day in his company. She just didn't know it yet.

Johara's assistants eyed him curiously, no doubt wondering why he was here, *again*. And why he didn't just walk right into his sister's office. That had been his first inclination, to corner that elusive elf in there.

He'd reconsidered. Raiding Kanza's leisure time was one thing. Marauding her at work was another. He'd let her get business out of the way before swooping in and sweeping her away on that day off Johara said she hadn't taken in over a year. He'd arranged a day off himself. The first whole one he'd had in…ever.

The office door was suddenly flung open, and Johara's head popped out, golden hair spilling forward. "Aram—come in, please."

He was on his feet at once, buoyed by the unexpected thrill of seeing Kanza now, not an hour or more later. "I thought you were having a meeting."

"When did that ever stop you?" Johara's grin widened as he ruffled her hair. "But as luck would have it, the day you chose to go against your M.O., I found myself in need of that incomparable business mind of yours, big brother."

He hugged her to his side, kissing the top of her head lovingly. "At your service always, sweetheart."

His gaze zeroed in on Kanza like a heat-seeking missile the moment he entered the office. Déjà vu spread its warmth inside his chest when he found her standing by the filing cabinets, like that first night. The only difference was the office was in pristine order. It had looked much better to him after she'd exercised her hurricane-like powers.

He noticed the other two people in the room only when they rose to salute him. All his faculties converged on that power source at the end of the office, even when he wasn't looking at her.

Then he did, and almost laughed out loud at the impact of her disapproving gaze and terse acknowledgment.

"Aram."

While it no longer sounded like a curse, it was…eloquent. No, more than that. Potent. Her unique, patented method of cutting him down to size.

Johara dragged back his attention, explaining their problem. Forcing himself to shift from Kanza to business mode, Aram turned to his sister's concerns.

After he'd gotten a handle on the situation, he offered solutions, only for Kanza to point out the lacking in some and the error in others. But she did so without the least contention or malice, as most would have when they considered someone to be infringing on their domain. In fact, there was nothing in her analysis except an earnest endeavor to reach the best possible solution.

Aram ascribed his lapse to close exposure to her, but he was lucid enough to know he was in the presence of a mind that rivaled his in his field. Having met only a handful of those in his lifetime, who'd been much older and wielding far more experience, he was beyond impressed.

As the session progressed, what impressed him even more was that she didn't compete with him, challenge him or harp on his early misjudgment. She deferred to his superior knowledge where he possessed it and put all her faculties at his disposal during what became five intensive hours of discussion, troubleshooting and restructuring.

Once they reached the most comprehensive plan of action, Johara leaped to her feet in excitement. "Fantastic! I couldn't have dreamed of such a genius solution! I should have teamed you and Kanza up a long time ago, Aram."

He couldn't believe it.

How had he not seen this as another of Johara's blatant efforts to show him how *compatible* they were? Would he *never* learn?

He twisted his lips at Johara for breaching their *noninterference* pact again as he rose to his feet. "And now that you did, how about we celebrate this breakthrough? It's on me."

Johara's eyes were innocence incarnate. "Oh, I wish. I have tons of boring, artistic stuff to take care of with Dana and Steve. You and Kanza go celebrate for us."

If anyone had told him before that business with Kanza that his kid sister was an ingenious actress, he wouldn't have believed it. But though he didn't approve of her underhanded methods, he was thankful for the opportunity she provided to get Kanza alone.

He turned to the little spitfire in question, gearing up for another battle, but Kanza simply said, "Let's go, then. I'm starving. And, Aram, it's on me. I owe you for those shortcuts you taught me today."

His head went light as the tension he'd gathered for the anticipated struggle drained out of him. Then it began to spin, at her admission that she'd learned from him, at her willingness to reward the favor.

Exchanging a last glance that no doubt betrayed his bewilderment with Johara, who was doing less than her usual seamless job of hiding her smug glee, he followed Kanza the Inscrutable out of the office.

Kanza walked out of Johara's office with the most disruptive force she'd ever encountered following her and a sense of déjà vu overwhelming her.

In the past two weeks he'd been taking this "get to know him" to the limit, had turned up everywhere to trail her as he was doing now. Instead of getting used to being inundated in his vibe and pervaded by his presence, each time the experience got more intense, had her reeling even harder.

And she still couldn't find one plausible reason why he was doing this.

The possibility that he was attracted to her had been the first one she'd dismissed. The idea of Aram Nazaryan, the epitome of male perfection, being romantically interested in her was so ludicrous it hadn't lasted more than two seconds of perplexed speculation before it had evaporated. Other reasons hadn't held water any better or longer.

So, by exclusion, one theory remained.

That he was nuts.

The hypothesis was loosely based on Johara's testimony.

With his repeated appearances of late, which Johara hadn't tied to Kanza, Johara had started talking about him. Among the tales from the past, mostly of their time in Zohayd, she'd let slip she believed he'd been sliding into depression. Kanza had barely held back from correcting Johara's tentative diagnosis to *manic*-depression, according to that inexplicable eagerness and elation that exuded from him and gleamed in his eyes.

Johara believed it was because he'd long been abusing his health and neglecting his personal life by working so much. Again, Kanza had barely caught back a scoff. In the past two weeks he hadn't seemed to work at all. How else could he turn up everywhere she went, no matter the time of day? Her only explanation was that he'd set up his business with such efficiency that its success was self-perpetuating and he could take time off whenever the fancy struck him.

But according to Johara, he had been working himself to death for years, resulting in being cut off from humanity and lately even becoming physically sick. It had been why she and Shaheen came so often to New York of late, staying for extended periods of time, to try to alleviate his isolation and stop his deterioration.

Not that Johara thought they were succeeding. She felt that their intimacy as husband and wife left Aram unable to connect with either of them as he used to, left him feeling like an outsider, even a trespasser. But she truly believed he needed the level of attachment he'd once shared with them to maintain his psychological health. Bottom line, she was worried that his inability to find anyone who fulfilled that need, along with his atrocious lifestyle, was dragging him to the verge of some breakdown.

But this man, stalking her like a panther who'd just discovered play and couldn't contain his eagerness to start a game of all-out tackle and chase, seemed nothing like the morose, self-destructive loner Johara had described. Which made *her* theory the only credible explanation. That his inexplicable pursuit of her was the first overt symptom of said breakdown.

Not that she was happy with this diagnosis.

While it had provided an explanation for his behavior, it had also influenced hers.

She'd dodged him so far, because she'd thought he'd

latched on to her in order to combat his ennui, and she hadn't fancied being used as an antidote to his boredom. But the idea that his behavior wasn't premeditated—or even worse, was a cry for help—had made it progressively harder to be unresponsive.

"So where do you want to take me?"

Doing her best not to swoon at the caress of his fathomless baritone, she turned to him as they entered the garage. "I'm open. What do you want to eat?"

"You pick." He grinned as he strode ahead, leading the way to his car. Seemed it was time for that spin in his nearsentient behemoth, a black-and-silver Rolls-Royce Phantom that reportedly came with a ghastly half-million-dollar price tag.

She stopped. "Okay, this goes no further."

That dazzling smile suddenly dimmed. "You're taking back your invitation?"

"I *mean* we're not going in circles, each insisting the other chooses. I already said I'm open to whatever you want, and it wasn't a ploy for you to throw the ball back in my court, proving you're more of a gentleman. I always say exactly what I mean."

His smile flashed back to its debilitating wattage. "You have no idea what a relief that is. But I'm definitely more of a gentleman. It's an incontestable anatomical fact."

She made no response as he seated her in his car's passenger seat. She wasn't going to take this exchange that lumped him and anatomy together any further. It would only lead to trouble.

Focusing instead on being in his car, she sank into the supple seashell leather while her feet luxuriated in the rich, thick lamb's wool, feeling cosseted in the literal lap of luxury.

After veering that impressive monster into downtown traffic, he turned to her. "So why did you suddenly stop evading me?"

Yeah. Good question. Why did she?

She told him the reason she'd admitted to herself so far. "I took pity on you."

"Yes." He pumped his fist. At her raised eyebrow, he chuckled. "Just celebrating the success of my pitiful puppy-dog-eyed efforts."

"If that's what you were shooting for, you missed the mark by a mile. You came across as a hyper, blazing-eyed panther."

Those eyes flared with enjoyment. "Back to the drawing board, then. Or rather the mirror, to practice. But if that didn't work…what did?"

And she found herself admitting more, to herself as well as to him. "It got grueling calculating the lengths you must have gone to, popping up wherever I went. It had me wondering if you're one of those anal-retentive people who must finish whatever they start, and I was needlessly prolonging both of our discomfort. I also had to see what would happen if I let go of the tug-of-war."

"You'll enjoy my company." At her sardonic sideways glance, he laughed. "Admit it. You find me entertaining."

She found him…just about everything.

"Not the adjective I'd use for you," Kanza said with a sigh.

"Don't leave me hanging. Lay it on me."

Her gaze lengthened over his dominant profile. She'd been candid in her description of his outward assets. Was it advisable to be her painfully outspoken self in expounding on what she thought of his more essential endowments?

Oh, what the hell. He must be used to fawning. Her truthfulness, though only her objective opinion, wouldn't be more than what he'd heard a thousand times before.

She opened her mouth to say she'd use adjectives like *enervating,* like a bolt of lightning, and *engulfing,* like a rising flood—and as if to say the words for her, thunder rolled and celestial floodgates burst.

He didn't press her to elucidate, because even with the efficiency of the automatic wipers, he could barely see through the solid sheets of rain. Thankfully, they seemed to have arrived at the destination he'd chosen. The Plaza Hotel, where Johara had mentioned Aram stayed.

As he stopped the car, she thought they should stay inside until the rain let up. They'd get soaked in the few dozen feet to the hotel entrance. Then he opened her door, and lo and behold...an umbrella was ingeniously embedded there. In moments, he was shielding her from the downpour and leading her through the splendor of the iconic hotel. But it wasn't until they stepped into the timeless Palm Court restaurant that she felt as if she'd walked into a scene out of *The Great Gatsby*.

She took in the details as she walked a step ahead among tables filled with immaculate people. Overhanging gilded chandeliers, paneled walls, a soaring twenty-foot green-painted and floral-patterned ceiling and 24-karat gold-leafed Louis XVI furniture, all beneath a stunning stained-glass skylight. Everything exuded the glamour that had made the hotel world famous while retaining the feel of a French country house.

After they were seated and she opted for ordering the legendary Plaza tea, she leveled her gaze back on him and sighed. "Is that your usual spending pattern? This hotel, that car?"

"I am moderate, aren't I?" At her grimace, he upped his teasing. "I was eyeing a Bugatti Veyron, but since there are no roads around to put it through its two-hundred-and-fifty-miles-per-hour paces, I thought paying three times as much as my current car would be unjustified." He chuckled at her growl of distaste. "Down, girl. I can afford it."

"And that makes it okay? Don't you have something better to do with your money?"

"I do a *lot* of better things with my money. And then, it's my only material indulgence. It's in lieu of a home."

"Meaning?"

"Meaning I've never bought a place, so I consider my cars my only home."

This was news. Somewhat...disturbing news. She'd thought he'd been staying in this hotel for convenience, not that he'd never had a place to call home.

"But...if you're saying you don't splurge on your accommodations, it would be *far* more economical—and an investment—to buy a place. A day here is an obscene amount of money down the drain, and you've been here almost a *year*."

His nod was serene. "My suite goes for about twenty grand a night." At her gasp, his lips spread wide. "Of which I'm not paying a cent. I am a major shareholder in this hotel, so I get to stay free."

Okay. She should have known a financial mastermind like him wouldn't throw money around, that he'd invest every cent to make a hundred. It was a good thing their orders had arrived so she'd have it instead of crow after she'd gone all self-righteous on him.

She felt him watching her and pretended to have eyes only on the proceedings as waiters heaped varieties of tea, finely cut sandwiches, scones, jam, clotted cream and a range of pastries on the table.

They had devoured two irresistible scones each, and mellow live piano music had risen above the buzz of conversation, when he broke the silence.

"This place reminds me of the royal palace in Zohayd. Not the architecture, but something in the level of splendor. The distant resemblance is...comforting."

The longing, the melancholy in his reminiscing about the place where he'd lived a good portion of his youth, tugged at her heart...a little too hard.

Suddenly his smile dawned again. "So ask me anything."

Struggling with the painful tautness in her throat, she eyed him skeptically. "Anything at all?"

His nod was instantaneous. "You bet."

It seemed Johara had been correct. He did need someone to share things with that he felt he could no longer share with his sister or brother-in-law. And as improbable as it was, he seemed to have elected her as the one he could unburden himself to. His selection had probably been based on her ability to say no to him, to be blunt with him. That must be a total novelty for him.

But she also suspected there was another major reason she was a perfect candidate for what he had in mind. Because he didn't seem to consider her a woman. Just a sexless buddy he could have fun with and confide in without worrying about the usual hassles a woman would cause him.

She had no illusions about what she was, how a man like him would view her. But that still had mortification warring with compassion in her already tight chest. Compassion won.

Feeling the ridiculous urge to reach across the table for his hand, to reassure him she was there for him, even if he thought her a sprite, she cleared her throat. "Tell me about the rift between you and Shaheen."

He nodded. "Did Johara tell you how we came to Zohayd?"

"Oh, no! You're planning to tell me your whole life story to get to one incident in its middle?"

"Yep. So you'll understand the factors leading up to the incident and the nature of the players in it."

"Can I retract my request?" She pretended glibness.

"Nope. *Dokhool el hammam mesh zay toloo'oh.*"

Entering a bathroom isn't like exiting it. What was said in Zohayd to signify that what was done couldn't be undone.

And she was beginning to realize what that really meant.

Living life knowing a man like him existed had been fine with her as long as he'd been just a general concept—not a reality that could cross hers, let alone invade it.

But now that she was experiencing him up close, she feared it would irrevocably change things inside her.

And the peace she'd once known would be no more.

Six

Pretending to eat what seemed to have turned to ashes, Kanza watched Aram as he poured her tea and began sharing his life story with her.

"Before I came to Zohayd at sixteen, my father used to whisk me, Johara and Mother away every year or so to yet another exotic locale as he built his reputation as an internationally rising jeweler. When I told my peers that I'd trade what they thought an enchanted existence in the glittering milieus of the rich and famous for a steady, boring life in a small town, dweeb and weirdo were only two of the names they called me. I learned to keep my mouth shut, but I couldn't learn to stop hating that feeling of homelessness. My defense was to go to any new place as if I was leaving the next day, and I remained in self-imposed isolation until we left."

She gulped scalding tea to swallow the lump in her throat. So his isolation had deeper roots than Johara even realized. And she'd bet she was the first one he'd told this to.

He went on. "I had a plan, though. That the moment I hit eighteen, I'd stay put in one place, work in one job forever, marry the first girl who wanted me and have a brood of kids. That blueprint for my future was what kept me going as the flitting around the world continued."

She gulped another mouthful, the heaviness in her chest increasing. His plans for stability had never come to pass. He was forty and as far as she knew, apart from the fiasco with Maysoon, he'd never had any kind of relationship.

So how had the one guy who'd planned a family life so early on, who'd craved roots when all others his age dreamed of freedom, ended up so adrift and alone?

He served them sandwiches and continued. "Then my father's mentor, the royal jeweler of Zohayd, retired and his job became open. He recommended Father to King Atef...."

Feeling as if a commercial had burst in during a critical moment, she raised a hand. "Hey, I'm from Zohayd and I know all the stories. How your father became the one entrusted with the Pride of Zohayd treasure is a folktale by now. Fast forward. Tell me something I don't know. I hate recaps."

His eyes crinkled at her impatience—he was clearly delighted she was so riveted by his story. "So there I was, jetting off to what Father said was one of the most magnificent desert kingdoms on earth, feeling resigned we'd stay for the prerequisite year before Father uprooted us again. Then we landed there. I can still remember, in brutal vividness, how I felt as soon as my feet touched the ground in Zohayd. That feeling of...belonging."

God. The emotions that suddenly blazed from him... Any moment now she was going to reach for that box of tissues.

"That feeling became one of elation, of certainty, that I'd found a home—that I *was* home—when I met Shaheen." His massive chest heaved as he released an unsteady breath. "Did Johara tell you how he saved her from certain death that day?"

She shook her head, her eyes beginning to burn.

"She was a hyperactive six-year-old who made me age

running after her. Then I take my eyes off her for a minute and she's dangling from the palace's balcony. I was too far away, and Father failed to reach her, and she was slipping. But then at the last second, Shaheen swooped in to snatch her out of the air like the hawk he's named after.

"I was there the next second, beside myself with fright and gratitude, and that kindred feeling struck me. And from that day forward, he became my first and only friend. As he became Johara's first and only love."

She let out a ragged breath. "Wow."

"Yeah." He leaned back in his chair. "It was indescribable, having the friendship of someone of Shaheen's caliber—a caliber that had nothing to do with his status. But though he felt just as closely bonded to me, considered me an equal, I knew the huge gap between us would always be unbridgeable. I grew more uncomfortable by the day when Johara started to blossom, and I became certain that her emotions for Shaheen weren't those of a friend but those of a budding woman in love.

"By the time she was fourteen, worry poisoned every minute I spent with Shaheen, which by then almost always included Johara. Though the three of us were magnificent together, I thought Shaheen's all-out indulgence of Johara would lead to catastrophe, for Johara, for my whole family. Then my anxiety reached critical mass…"

"Go on," she rasped when he paused, unable to wait to hear the rest.

He raked a hand through his dark, satin hair. "We were having a squash match, and I started to trounce a bewildered Shaheen. The more Johara cheered him to fight back, the more vicious I became. Afterward in the changing room, I tore into Shaheen with all my pent-up resentment. I called him a spoiled prince who made a game of manipulating people's emotions. I accused him of encouraging her crush on him—which he knew was beyond hopeless—just for fun. I demanded he stop leading her on or I'd tell his father King Atef...so he'd *order* him never to come near Johara again.

"Shaheen was flabbergasted. He said Johara was the little sister he'd never had. I only sneered that his affections went far beyond an older brother's, as I should know as her *real* one. He countered that while he didn't know what having a sister was like, Johara was his 'girl'—the one who 'got' him like no one else, even me, and he did love her... in every way but *that* way.

"But I was way beyond reason, said that his proclamations meant nothing to me—I cared only about Johara—and that he was emotionally exploiting her, and I wouldn't stand idly by waiting for him to damage her irrevocably."

She couldn't imagine how he'd felt at the time. Sensing the powerful bond between his best friend and sister, having every reason to believe it would end in devastation and being forced to risk his one friendship to protect his one sister. It must have been terrible, knowing that either way he'd lose something irreplaceable.

Grimacing with remembered pain, Aram placed his forearms on the table, his gaze fixed on the past. "Outrage finally overpowered Shaheen's mortification that I could think such dishonorable things of him. His bitterness escalated as my conviction faltered, then vanished in the face of his intense affront and hurt. But there was no taking back what I'd said or threatened. Then it was too late, anyway.

"Shaheen told me he'd save me the trouble of running to his father with my demands for him to cease and desist. He'd never come near Johara again. Or me. He carried out his pledge, cutting Johara and me off, effective immediately."

It was clear the injury of those lost years had never fully healed. And though Shaheen and Johara were now happily married and Aram's friendship with Shaheen had been restored, it seemed the gaping wound where his friend had been torn out had been only partially patched. Because there was no going back to the same closeness now that Shaheen's life was so full of Johara and their daughter while Aram had found nothing to fill the void in his own life. Except work. And according to Johara, it was nowhere near enough.

"Just when I thought Shaheen's alienation was the worst thing that could happen to me, Mother suddenly took Johara and left Zohayd. I watched our family being torn apart and was unable to stop it. Then I found myself left alone with a devastated father who kept withdrawing into himself in spite of all my efforts. I tried to grope for my best friend's support, hoping he'd let me close again, but he only left Zohayd, too, dashing any hope for a reconciliation."

So she had been totally wrong about him in this instance, too. It hadn't been not caring that had caused that breach; it had been caring too much. And it had cost him way more than she'd ever imagined.

He went on. "With all my dreams of making a home for myself in Zohayd over, I wanted to leave and tried to persuade Father to leave with me, too, but I backed off when I realized his service to the king and kingdom was what kept him going. Knowing I couldn't leave him, I resigned myself that I'd stay in Zohayd as long as he lived."

It must have been agonizingly ironic to get what he wanted, that permanent stay in Zohayd, but for it to be more of an exile than a home.

As if he'd heard her thoughts, he released a slow, deep breath. "It was the ultimate irony. I was getting what I'd hoped for all my life—stability in one place, just without the roots or the family, to live there in an isolation that promised to become permanent." *Isolation.* There was that word again. "Then, six years after everyone left Zohayd, I took a shot at forging that family I'd once dreamed of…and you now know what happened next."

She nodded, her throat tight. "And you ended up being forced to leave."

He sighed deeply again. "Yeah. So much happened after

that. Too much. And I've never stayed in one place longer than a few months since. I hadn't wanted to. Couldn't bear to, even. Then three years ago, Shaheen and Johara ended up getting married. I was right about the nature of their involvement." He smiled whimsically. "I just jumped the gun by twelve years." Another deep sigh. "Then suddenly I had my friend back, Mother reconciled with Father and my whole family was put back together—just in Zohayd, where I could no longer be."

Swallowing what felt like a rock, she wondered if he'd elaborate on the intervening years, the "too much" he'd said with such aversion. He didn't.

He'd done what he'd set out to do, told her the story that explained his rift with Shaheen. Anything else would be for another day. If there would be one.

From the way her heart kept twisting, it wasn't advisable to have one. Exposure to him when she'd despised him, thought him a monster, had been bad enough. Now that she saw him as not only human but even empathetic, further exposure could have catastrophic consequences. For her.

His eyes seemed to see her again, seeming to intensify in vividness as he smiled like never before. A heartfelt smile.

"Thank you."

Her heart fired so hard it had her sitting forward in her chair. "Wh-what for?"

The gentleness turning his beauty from breathtaking to heartbreaking deepened. "You listened. And made no judgments. I think you even…sympathized."

She struggled to stop the pins at the back of her eyes from dissolving in an admission of how moved she was. "I did. It was such a tragic and needless waste, all those years apart. For all of you."

His inhalation was sharp. The exhalation that followed was slow, measured. "Yes. But they're back together now."

They. Not we.

He didn't seem to consider he had his family and friend

back. Worse, it seemed he didn't consider himself part of the family anymore. And though his expression was now carefully neutral, she sensed he was...desolate over the belief. What he seemed to consider an unchangeable fact of his life now.

After that, as if by unspoken agreement, they spent the rest of their time in the Palm Court talking about a dozen things that weren't about lost years or ruined life plans.

After the rain stopped, he took her out walking, and they must have covered all of Central Park before it was dark.

She didn't even feel the distance, the exertion or the passage of time. She saw nothing, heard and smelled and felt nothing but him. His company was that engrossing, that gratifying. The one awful thing about spending time with him was that it would come to an end.

But it didn't. When she'd thought their impromptu outing was over, he insisted she wasn't going home until she was a full, exhausted mass unable to do anything but fall into bed. She hadn't even thought of resisting his unilateral plans for the rest of the evening. This time out of time would end soon enough, and she wasn't going to terminate it prematurely. She'd have plenty of time later to regret her decision not to.

Over dinner, their conversation took a turn for the funny, then the hilarious. On several occasions, his peals of goosebump-raising laughter incited many openmouthed and swooning stares from besotted female patrons, while *she* was leveled with what's-*she*-doing-with-that-god glares, not to mention the times the whole restaurant seemed to be turning around to see if there was a hyena dining with them.

When he drove her back to her apartment building, he parked two blocks away—just an excuse to have another walk.

As they walked in companionable silence, she felt the impulsive urge to hook her arm in his, lean on him through

the wind. It wasn't discretion that stopped her but the fact
that he hadn't attempted even a courteous touch so far.

At her building's entrance, he turned to her with expecta-
tion blazing in those azure eyes. "So same time tomorrow?"

Her heart pirouetted in her chest at the prospect of another day with him.

But… "We went out at *one* today!"

He shrugged. "And?"

"And I have work."

He waved dismissively. "Take the day off."

"I can't. Johara…"

"Will shove you out of the office if she can to make you
take some time off. She says you're a workaholic."

"Gee. She says the same about you."

"See? We both need a mental-health day."

"We already had one today."

"We worked our asses off for five hours in the morning.
Tomorrow is a *real* day off. With all the trimmings. Sleeping in, then going crazy being lazy and doing nothing but
eating and chatting and doing whatever pops into our minds
till way past midnight."

And he'd just described her newfound vision of heaven.

Then she remembered something, and heaven seemed to
blink out of sight. She groaned, "I really can't tomorrow."

Disappointment flooded his gaze, but only for a second.
Then eagerness was back full steam ahead. "The day after
tomorrow, then. And at noon. No…make it eleven. *Ten.*"

Her heart tap-danced. She did her best not to grin like
a loon, to sound nonchalant as she said, "Oh, all right."

He stuck his hands at his hips. "Got something more en-
thusiastic than that?"

"Nope." She mock scowled. "That's the only brand available. Take it or…take it."

"I'll take it, and take it!" He took a step back as if to
dodge a blow, whistled. "Jeez. How did something so tiny
become so terrifying?"

She gave a sage nod. "It's an evolutionary compensatory mechanism to counteract the disadvantaged size."

"Vive la évolution." And he said it in perfect French, reminding her he spoke that fluently, too.

She burst out laughing.

Minutes later, she was still chuckling to herself as she entered her apartment. God, but that man was the most unprecedented, unpredictable, unparalleled fun she'd ever had.

She met her eyes in her foyer's mirror, wincing at what she'd never seen reflected back...until now. Unmistakable fever in her cheeks and soppy dreaminess in her eyes. Aram had put it all there without even meaning to.

Yeah. He was boatloads of fun. Too bad he was also a mine of danger.

And she'd just agreed to another daylong dose of deadly exposure.

Seven

"So how's my Tiny Terror doing this fine day?"

Kanza leaned against the wall to support legs that always went elastic on hearing Aram's voice. Not to mention the heart that forgot its rhythm.

You'd think after over a month of daily and intensive exposure, she'd have developed some immunity. But she only seemed to be getting progressively more susceptible.

She forced out a steady, "Why, thank you, I'm doing splendidly. And you, Hulking Horror?"

Right on cue, his expected laugh came, boisterous and unfettered. He kept telling her that she had the specific code that operated his humor, and almost everything she said tickled him mercilessly. She'd been liberally exercising that power over him, to both their delight.

In return, the gift of his laughter, and knowing that she could incite it, caused her various physical and emotional malfunctions.

She was dealing with the latest bout when he said, laughter still permeating his magnificent voice, "I'm doing spectacularly now that my Mighty Miniature has taken me well in hand. You ready? I'm downstairs." Yeah, he never even asked to come up. "And hurry! I have something to show you."

"Uh-uh. Don't play that game with me." She took a look in the mirror and groaned. Not a good idea to inspect herself right before she beheld him. The comparison was just too disheartening. She slammed out of her apartment in frustration and ran into the elevator that a neighbor had just exited. "Tell me what it is. I have severe allergies to surprises."

"Just so we won't end up in the E.R., I'll give you a hint." His voice had that vibrant edge of excitement she'd been hearing more of late as they planned trips they'd take and projects they'd do together. "It's things people live in."

Her heart sputtered in answering excitement. "You bought an apartment! Oh, congrats."

"Hey, you think me capable of making a decision without consulting my Mini Me?"

The elevator opened to reveal him. And it hit her all over again with even more force than last time. How…shattering his beauty was.

But with the evidence of his current glory, she knew he'd been right. When she'd met him again six weeks ago, he *had* been at his lowest ebb. Ever since then, he'd been steadily shedding any sign of haggardness. He was now at a level that should be prohibited by law, like any other health hazard.

And there she was, the self-destructive fool who willingly exposed herself to his emanations on a daily basis. And without any protection.

Not that there was any, or that she'd want it if there was. She'd decided to open herself up to the full exposure and to hell with the certain and devastating side effects.

As usual, without even taking her arm or touching her in any way whatsoever, he rushed ahead, gesturing eagerly for her to follow. She did. As she knew by now, she always would.

Once in his car and on their way, he turned to her. "I'm

taking you to see the candidates. I'm signing the contract of the one you'll determine I'll feel most comfortable in."

Her jaw dropped. "And I'm supposed to know that... how?"

His sideways glance was serenity itself. "Because you know everything."

"Hey." She turned in her seat. "Thanks for electing me your personal oracle or goddess or whatever, but no thanks. You can't saddle me with this kind of responsibility."

"It's your right and prerogative, O Diminutive Deity."

She rolled her eyes. "What ever happened to free will?"

"Who needs that when I have you?"

"If it was anyone else, I'd be laughing. But I know you're crazy enough to sign a contract if I as much as say a word in preference of one place." His nod reinforced her projection. "What if you end up hating my choice?"

"I won't." His smile was confidence incarnate. "And that's not crazy, but the logical conclusion to the evidence of experience. Everything you choose for me or advise me to do turns out to be the perfect solution for me. Case in point, look at me."

And she'd been trying her best not to. Not to stare, anyway. He gestured at his clothes. "You pointed this out in a shop yesterday, said I'd look good in it."

Yeah, because you'd look good in anything. You'd make a tattered sac look like haute couture.

"Even though I thought I'd look like a cyanotic parrot in this color..." A deep, intense purple that struck incredible hues off his hair and eyes. "I bought it on the way here based solely on your opinion. Now I think I've never worn anything more complimenting."

Her lips twisted in mockery, and with a twinge at how right he was. He looked the most vital and incandescent he'd ever been. "Pink frills would compliment you, Aram."

"Then I'll try those next."

A chuckle overpowered her as imaginings flooded her mind. "God, this I have to see."

His grin flashed, dazzling her. "Then you will." Suddenly his face settled into a seriousness that was even more hard-hitting. "All joking aside, I'm not being impulsive here. I'm a businessman, and I make my decisions built on what works best. And *you* work best."

"Uh, thanks. But in exactly what way do I do that?"

"Your perception is free from the distortions of inclinations. You cut to the essence of things, see people and situations for what they are, not what you'd prefer them to be, and don't let the background noise of others' opinions distract you." He slid her that proud, appreciative glance that he bestowed on her so frequently these days. "You proved that to me when you accepted my word and adjusted your opinion of me, guided only by your reading of me against overwhelming circumstantial evidence and long-standing misconceptions. It's because you're so welcoming of adjustments and so goal oriented that you achieve the best results in everything. I mean, look at me…"

Oh, God, not again. Didn't he have any idea what it did to her just being near him, let alone looking more closely at him than absolutely necessary?

No, he didn't.

He had no idea whatsoever how he made her feel.

She sighed. "I'm looking. And purple does become you. Anything else I should be looking at?"

"Yes, the miracle you worked. You took a fed-up man who was feeling a hundred years old and turned him into that eager kid who skips around doing all the things he'd long given up on. And you did it by just being your no-nonsense self, by just reading me right and telling me everything you thought and exactly what I have to hear."

She almost winced. She wasn't telling *everything* she thought. Not by a long shot. But her thoughts and feelings where he was concerned were her responsibility. She had no right to burden him with what didn't concern him.

But he was making it harder by the minute to contain those feelings within her being's meager boundaries.

He wasn't finished with his latest bout of unwitting torment. "You yanked me out of the downward spiral I was resigned to plunge into until I hit rock bottom. So, yes, I'm sure your choice of abodes will be the best one for me. Because you've been the best thing that has ever happened to me."

The heart that had been squeezing harder with every incredible word almost burst.

To have him so eloquently reinforcing her suspicion that he'd come to consider her the replacement best friend/sister he needed was both ecstasy and agony.

Feeling the now-familiar heat simmering behind her eyes, she attempted to take this back to lightness. "What's with the seriousness? And here I was secure in the fact that you're incapable of being that way around me."

His smile was so indulgent that she felt something coming undone right in her very essence. "I'm always serious around you. Just in a way that's the most fun I've ever had. But if you feel I'm burdening you with making this choice…"

And she had to laugh. "Oh, shut up, you gigantic weasel. After all the sucking up you did, and all the puppy-dog-eyed persuasion that you *have* perfected in front of that mirror, you have the audacity to pretend that I have a choice here?"

His guffaw belted out, almost made her collapse onto herself. "Ah, Kanza, *you* are the most fun I've ever had."

Yeah. What every girl wanted to hear from the most divine man on earth. That she made him laugh.

But she'd already settled for that. For anything with him. For as long as she could have it. Come what may.

He brought the car to a stop in front of a building that felt vaguely familiar. As he opened his door, she jumped out so he wouldn't come around to open hers, since opening doors and pulling back seats for her seemed to be the only acts that indicated that he considered her female.

When he fell into step beside her, she did a double take.

They were on Fifth Avenue. Specifically in front of one of the top Italian-renaissance palazzo-style apartment buildings in Manhattan.

Forgetting everything but the excitement of apartment hunting, she turned to him with a whoop. "I used to live a block from here." And she'd found the area only "vaguely familiar." He short-circuited her brain even more than she'd thought. "God, I loved that apartment. It was the only place that ever felt like home."

His eyebrows shot up. "Zohayd didn't feel like that?"

"Not really. You know what it was like."

He frowned and, if possible, became more edible than ever. "Actually, I have no idea how it was like for you there. Because you never told me." As soon as they entered the elevator, he turned to her with a probing glance. "How did we never get to talk about your life in Zohayd?"

She shrugged. "Guess we had more important things to discuss. Like how to pick the best avocado."

His lips pursed in displeasure. "That alone makes me realize how remiss I've been and that there is a big story here. One I won't rest until I hear."

She waved him off. "It's boring, really."

His pout was adamant. "I live to be bored by you."

The last thing she wanted to do was tell him about her disappointment-riddled life in Zohayd. But knowing him, he'd persist until she told him. The best she could hope for was to distract him for now.

She took the key from his hand as they got off the elevator. "Which apartment?"

He pointed out the one at the far end of the floor.

As they sauntered in that direction, he looked down at her. "So about this old place of yours—if it felt like home, and I'm assuming your new place doesn't, why did you move?"

"A friend from Zohayd begged me to room with her, as she couldn't live alone, and the new place was right by her work. Then she up and got married on me and went back to Zohayd, and I never got around to going back to my place. But now that you might be buying a place this close, it would save us a lot of commuting if I got it back. Hope it's still on the market."

"Choose this apartment, and I'll *make* it on the market."

"Oh. Watch out, world, for the big, bad tycoon. He snaps his fingers and the market yelps and rolls over."

He gave her a deep bow. "At your service."

They laughed and exchanged wit missiles as they entered the opulent duplex through a marble-framed doorway. Then she fell silent as she beheld what looked straight out of the pages of *Architectural Digest*. Sweeping, superbly organized layouts with long galleries, an elegant staircase, lush finishes, oversize windows, high ceilings and a spacious terrace that wrapped around two sides of the apartment. It was even furnished to the highest standards she'd ever seen and very, very much to her taste.

In only minutes of looking around, she turned to Aram. "Okay, no need to see anything more. Or any other place. I hereby proclaim that you will find utmost comfort here."

He again bowed deeply, azure flames of merriment leaping in his eyes. "My Minuscule Mistress, thy will be done."

And in the next hour, it was. He immediately called the Realtor, who zoomed over with the contracts. Aram passed them to her to read before he signed, and she made some amendments before giving him the green light. From then on, it took only minutes for the check to be handed over and the Realtor to leave the apartment almost bouncing in delight.

Aram came back from walking the lady to the front door, his smile flooding his magnificent new place in its radiance.

"Now to inaugurate the apartment with our first meal." He threw himself down beside her on the elegant couch. "So what are we eating?"

She cocked an eyebrow at him and tsked. "This inability to make decisions without my say-so is becoming worrisome."

He slid down farther on the couch, reclining his big, powerful body more comfortably. "I've been making business decisions for countless employees, clients and shareholders for the past eight years. I'm due for a perpetual vacation from making minor- to moderate-sized decisions for the rest of my personal life."

She gave him her best stern scowl, which she resignedly knew he thought was the most adorable thing ever. "And I'm the one who's supposed to pick up the slack and suddenly be responsible for your decisions as well as mine?"

He nodded in utmost complacency. "You do it so well, so naturally. And it's your fault. You're the one who got me used to this." His gaze became that cross between cajoling and imploring that he'd perfected. "You're not leaving me in the lurch now, are you?"

"Stop with the eyes!" she admonished. "Or I swear I'll blindfold you."

"What a brilliant idea. Then besides making decisions for me, you'll have to lead me around by the hand. Even more unaccountability for me to revel in."

She threw her hands up. "Sushi, okay. Here's your decision before I find myself taking over your business, too, while you go indulge in the teenage irresponsibility you evidently never had."

Chuckling, he got out his phone. Then he proceeded to ask her exactly what kind of sushi they were eating, piece by piece, until she had to slam him with a cushion.

After they'd wiped off the delicious feast, he was pouring her jasmine tea when she noticed him looking at her in an even more unsettling, contemplative way.

"What?" she croaked.

"I was wondering if you were always this interesting."

"And I'm wondering if you were always this condescending. Oh, wait, you were even worse. You used to look at me like I was a strange life-form."

"You *were* a strange life-form. I mean, green body makeup? And pink contacts? Pink? Did you have those custom-made?" He rejoined her on the couch with his own cup. "What statement were you making?"

She was loath to remember those times when she'd felt alone even while deluged by people. When she used to look at him and know that *nogoom el sama a'arablaha*—that the stars in the sky were closer than he was. Now, though he was a breath away, he remained as distant, as impossible to reach.

She sighed, shaking free from the wave of melancholy. "One of my stepmothers, Maysoon's mother, popularized Kanza the Monster's name until everyone was using it. So I decided to go the whole hog and look the part."

His eyes went grim, as if imagining having his hands on those who'd been so inconsiderate with her. Knowing him, she didn't put it past him that he would act on his outrage on behalf of her former self.

"What made you give it up?" His voice was dark with barely suppressed anger. "Then go all the way in the other direction, doing without any sort of enhancement?"

She shrugged. "I developed an allergy to makeup."

His lips twitched as his anger dissolved into wry humor. "Another allergy?"

"Not a real one. I just realized that regardless of whether makeup makes me look worse or better, I was focusing too much on what others thought of me. So I decided to focus on myself. Be myself."

That pride he showered on her flooded his gaze. "Good for you. You're perfect just the way you are."

Kanza stared at him. In any romantic movie, as the hero

professed those words, he would have suddenly seen his dorky best friend in a new light, would have realized she was beautiful in his eyes and that he wanted her for more than just a friend.

Before her heart imploded with futility, she slid down on the couch, pretending she thought it a good moment for one of those silent rituals they exercised together.

Inside her, there was only cacophony.

Aram considered her perfect.

Just not for him.

Eight

Aram sank further into tranquility and relaxation beside Kanza, savoring the companionable silence they excelled at together, just as they did at exhilarating repartee.

Just by being here, she'd turned this place, which he'd felt ambivalent toward until she'd entered it and decided she liked it, into a home. He'd decided to have one at last only because she'd said she would always stay in New York and make it hers.

He sighed, cherishing the knowledge that expanded inside him with each passing hour.

She was really her name. A treasure.

And to think that no one, even Shaheen and Johara, realized how much of one she really was.

He guessed she was too different, too unexpected, too unbelievable for others to be able to fathom, let alone to handle.

She was perfect to him.

It was hard to believe that only six weeks ago he hadn't had her in his life. It felt as if his existence had *become* a life only once she'd entered it.

And it seemed like a lifetime ago when Shaheen had

suggested her as a convenient bride, convinced she'd consider his assets and agree to the arrangement. If Shaheen only knew her, he would have known that she'd sign a contract of enslavement before she would a marriage of convenience. If he'd known how unique, how exceptional she was, he wouldn't have even thought of such an unworthy fate for her.

She'd achieved her success in pursuit of self-realization and accomplishment, not status and wealth—things she cared nothing about and would certainly never wish to attain through a man. She'd even made it clear she didn't consider marriage a viable option for herself. But among the many misconceptions about her had been his own worry that his initial fascination would fade, and she'd turn out to be just another opportunistic woman who'd use any means necessary to reel in a husband.

But the opposite had happened. His fascination, his admiration, his pleasure at being with her intensified by the minute. For the first time, he found himself attracted to the *whole* woman, his attraction not rooted in sexuality or sustained by it. He had to use Shaheen's word to describe what they were. Compatible. They were matched on every level—personally, professionally, mentally and emotionally. Her every quality and skill meshed with and complemented his own. She was his equal, and his superior in many areas.

She was *just* perfect.

Just yesterday, Shaheen had asked him for an update on whether he'd changed his mind about Kanza now that he'd gotten to know her.

He'd said only that he had, leaving it at that.

What he'd really meant was that he had changed his mind about *everything*.

The more he was with Kanza, the more everything he'd believed of himself—of his limits, inclinations, priorities and everything he'd felt before her—changed beyond all recognition.

She made him work hard for her respect and esteem, for the pleasure and privilege of his presence in her life, for her gracing his with hers. She gave him what no one had ever given him before, not even Shaheen or Johara. She *reveled* in being with him as much as he did with her. She *got* him on every level. She accepted him, challenged him, and when she felt there were things about him that needed fixing— and there were *many*—she just reached inside him with the magic wand of her candor and caring and put it right.

She'd turned his barren existence into a life of fulfillment, every day bringing with it deeper meanings, invigorating discoveries and uplifting experiences.

The only reason he'd fleetingly considered Shaheen's offer had been for the possibility of filling his emptiness with a new purpose in life and the proximity of his family. Now he found little reason to change his status quo. For what could possibly be better than this?

It was just perfection between them.

So when Shaheen had asked for an update, really asking about projected developments, he couldn't bear thinking of any. How could he when any might tamper with this blissful state? He was *terrified* anything would happen to change it.

They were both unconcerned about the world and its conventions, and things were flourishing between them. He only hoped they would continue to deepen in the exact same way. So even if he wanted to, he certainly wasn't introducing any new variable that might fracture the flawlessness.

For now, the only change he wanted to introduce was removing the last barrier inside him. He wanted to let her into his being, fully and totally.

So he did. "There's something I haven't told you yet. Something nobody knows."

She turned to him, her glorious mass of hair rustling as if it was alive, those unique obsidian eyes delving deep inside his recesses, letting him know she was there for him always.

Just gazing into them he felt invincible. And secure that he could share everything with her, even his shame.

"It happened a few months after I left Zohayd...." He paused, the long-repressed confession searing out of his depths. He braced himself against the pain, spit it out. "I got involved in something...that turned out to be illegal, with very dangerous people. I ended up in prison."

That had her sitting up. And what he saw on her face rocked through him. Instantaneous reassurance that, whatever had happened, whatever he told her, it wouldn't change her opinion of him. She was on his side. Unequivocally.

And as he'd needed to more frequently of late, he took a moment to suppress the desire to haul her to him and crush her in the depths of his embrace with all his strength.

The need to physically express his feelings for her had been intensifying every day. But she'd made no indication that she'd accept that. Worse. She didn't seem to want it.

It kept him from initiating anything, even as much as a touch. For what if even a caress on her cheek or hair changed the dynamic between them? What if it made her uneasy and put her on her guard around him? What if he then couldn't take it back and convince her that he'd settle for their previous hands-off status quo, forever if need be?

He brought the urge under control with even more difficulty than he had the last time it had assailed him, his voice sounding as harsh as broken glass as he went on, "I was sentenced to three years. I was paroled after only one."

Her solemn eyes were now meshed with his. He felt he was sinking into the depths of their unconditional support, felt understood, cosseted, protected. It was as if she was reaching to him through time, to offer him her strength to tide him through the incarceration, to soothe the wounds and erase his scars.

"For good behavior?" Her voice was the gentlest he'd ever heard it.

He barked a mirthless laugh. "Actually, they probably

wanted me out to get rid of me. I was too much trouble, gave them too many inmates to patch up. I almost killed a couple. I spent over nine months of that year in solitary. The moment they let me out, I put more inmates in the infirmary and I was shoved back there."

"You ended up being…solitary too many times throughout your life."

She'd mused that as if to herself. But he felt her soft, pondering words reaching down inside him to tear out the talons he'd long felt sunk into his heart. Making him realize that it hadn't been the solitude itself that had eaten at him but the notion that he'd never stop being alone.

But now she was here, and he'd never be alone again.

Her smile suddenly dawned, and it lit up his entire world. "But you still managed to make the best of a disastrous situation in your own inimitable way."

"It wasn't only my danger to criminal life-forms that got me out. I was a first-time offender, and I was lucky to find people who believed that I had made a mistake, not committed a crime. Those allies helped me get out, and afterward, they supported my efforts to…expunge my record."

The radiance of her smile intensified, scorching away any remnants of the ordeal's despondency and indignity. "So you're an old hand at expunging your record. And I wasn't the first one who believed in you."

He didn't know how he stopped himself from grabbing her hands, burying his lips and face in them, grabbing *her* and burying his whole being in her magnanimity and faith.

He expended the urge on a ragged breath. "You're the first and only one who did with only the evidence of my word."

She waved that away. "As you so astutely pointed out the first night, I do know Maysoon. That was a load of evidence in your favor, once I'd heard both sides of the story."

He wasn't about to accept her qualification. "No. You

employed this unerring truth-and-justice detector of yours without any backing evidence. You read *me*. You believed *me*."

Her eyes gleamed with that indulgence that melted him to his core. "Okay, okay, I did. Boy, you're pushy."

"And you believed me again now," he insisted, needing to hear her say it. "When I said I didn't knowingly commit a crime, even when I gave you no details, let alone evidence."

Teasing ebbed, as if she felt he needed the assurance of her seriousness. "Yes, I did, because I know you'd always tell me the truth, the bad before the good. If you'd been guilty, you would have told me. Because you know I can't accept anything but the truth and because you know that whatever it was, it wouldn't make a difference to me."

Hot thorns sprouted behind his eyes, inside his heart. Everything inside him surged, needing to mingle with her.

He had to end these sublime moments before he...expressed how moved he was by them, shattering them instead.

He first had to try to tell her what her belief meant to him. "Your trust in me is a privilege and a responsibility that I will always nurture with pride and pleasure."

Her gaze suddenly escaped his, flowed down his body.

By the time they rose back, he was hard all over. Thankfully, her eyes were intent on his, full of contemplation.

"Though you're so big, with no doubt proportionate strength, it never occurred to me you'd be that capable of physical violence."

The vice that had released his heart suddenly clamped around it again. "Does this...disturb you?"

Her laugh rang out. "Hello? Have you met me? It *thrills* me. I would have loved to see you decimate a few thugs and neuter some bullies."

His hands, his whole being itched, ached. He just wanted to squeeze the hell out of her. He wanted to contain her, assimilate her and never let her go again.

He again held back with all he had, then drawled, "And to think something so minuscule could be so bloodthirsty."

She grinned impishly. "You've got a lot to learn about just what this deceptive exterior hides, big man."

Though her words tickled him and her smile was unfettered, he was still unsettled. "Is it really no problem for you to change your perception of me from someone who's too civilized to use his brute strength to someone who relishes physical violence?"

She shook her head, her long, thick hair falling over her slight shoulders down to her waist. "I don't believe you 'relish' it, but you'll always do 'what works best.' At the time, violence was the one thing that would keep the sharks away. So you used it, and to maximum efficiency, as is your way with everything. I'm only lamenting that there's no video documentation of those events for *me* to cheer over."

The delight she always struck in his heart overflowed in an unbridled guffaw. "I can just see you, grabbing the popcorn and hollering at the screen for more gore. But I might be able to do something about your desire to see me on a rampage. I can pull some strings at the prison and get some surveillance-camera footage."

She jumped up to her knees on the couch, nimble and keen as a cat. "Yes, yes, please!"

"Uh…I'm already regretting making the offer. You might think you can withstand what you'd see, but it was no staged fight like those you see on TV. There was no showmanship involved, just brutality with only the intent to survive at whatever cost."

She tucked her legs as if she was starting a meditation session, her gaze ultraserious. "That only makes it even more imperative to see it, Aram. It was the ugliest, harshest, most humiliating test you've ever endured and your deepest scar. I need to experience it in more than imagination, even if in the cold distance of past images, so I'd be able to share it with you in the most profound way I need to."

Stirred through to his soul, he swallowed a jagged lump of gratitude. "You just have to want it and it's done."

"Oh, I so want it. Thank you." Before he pounced with a thank-*you,* she probed, "You've really been needing to confide this all this time. Why didn't you?"

She was killing him with her ability to see right into his depths. She was reviving him with it, reanimating him.

"I was…ashamed. Of my weakness and stupidity. I wanted to prove to Shaheen and his brothers that I didn't need their help after all, that I'd make it on my own. And I got myself involved in something that looked too good to be true because I was in such a hurry to do it. And I paid the price."

She tilted her head to the side, as if to look at him from another perspective. "I can't even imagine what it was like. When you were arrested, when you were sentenced, when you realized you might have destroyed your future, maybe even tainted that of your family. That year in prison…"

He wanted to tell her that she was imagining it just fine, that her compassion was dissipating the lingering darkness of that period, erasing the scars it had left behind. But his throat was closed, his voice gone.

The empathy in her gaze rose until it razed him. "But I can understand the ordeal was a link in the chain that led to your eventual decline. Not the experience itself as much as the reinforcement of your segregation. You couldn't share such a life-changing experience with your loved ones, mainly because you wanted to protect them from the agony they would have felt on your behalf. But that very inability to bare your soul to them made you pull further away emotionally, and actually exacerbated your solitude."

When he finally found his voice, it was a hoarse, ragged whisper. "See? You do know everything."

Her eyes gentled even more. "Not everything. I'm still unable to fill some spaces. You were going strong for years after your imprisonment. Was that only *halawet el roh?*"

Literally sweetness of the soul. What was said in Zohayd to describe a state of deceptive vigor, a clinging to life when warding off inevitable deterioration or death.

"Now that you mention it, that's the best explanation. I came out of prison with a rabid drive to wipe out what happened, to right my path, to make up for lost time. I guess I was trying to run hard and fast enough to escape the memories, to accumulate enough success and security to fix the chasm the experience had ripped inside me and that threatened to tear me open at any moment."

Her eyes now soothed him, had him almost begging her to let her hand join in their caress. "Johara told me you were at the peak of fitness, at least physically, three years ago when you attended their wedding in Zohayd. From her observations, you started deteriorating about two years ago. Was there a triggering event? Like when it sank in that they were a family now? Did their togetherness—especially with your parents' reconciliation—leave you feeling more alone than ever?"

He squeezed his eyes on a spasm of poignancy. "You get me so completely. You get me better than I get myself."

Wryness touched her lips. "It was Johara who gave me the code to decipher your hieroglyphics when she said she felt as if her and Shaheen's intimacy left you unable to connect with either of them on the same level as you used to."

"She's probably right. But it's not only my own hang-ups. Neither of them has enough left to devote to anyone else. A love like that fills up your being. And then there's the massive emotional investment in Gharam and their coming baby."

Something inscrutable came into her eyes, intensifying their already absolute darkness.

Seeming to shake herself out of it, whatever it was, she continued searching his recesses. "So *was* there a triggering physical event? That made your health start to deteriorate?"

"Nothing specific. I just started being unable to sleep

well, to eat as I should. Everything became harder, took longer and I did it worse. Then each time I got even a headache or caught a cold, it took me ages to bounce back. My focus, my stamina, my immunity were just shot. I guess my whole being was disintegrating."

"But you're back in tip-top shape now."

It was a question, not a statement, worry tingeing it.

He let his gaze cup her elfin face in lieu of his hands. "I've never been better. And it's thanks to you."

Her smile faltered as she again waved his assertion away. "There you go again, crediting me with miracles."

"You *are* a miracle. My Minute Miracle. Not that size has anything to do with your effect. *That's* supreme."

He jumped to his feet, feeling younger and more alive than he'd ever felt, needing to dive headfirst into the world, doing everything under the sun with her. He rushed to fetch their jackets, then dashed back to her. "Let's go run in the rain. Then let's hop on my jet and go have breakfast anywhere you want. Europe. South America. Australia. Anywhere."

She donned her jacket and ran after him out of the apartment with just as much zeal. "How about the moon?"

Delighted at her willingness to oblige him in whatever he got it in his mind to say or do, he said, "If it's what you want, then I'll make it happen."

She pulled one of those funny faces that he adored. "And I wouldn't put it past you, too. Nah…I'll settle for something on terra firma. And close by. I have to work in the morning, even if you're so big and important now you no longer have to."

He consulted his watch. "If we leave for Barbados in an hour, I'll have you at work by ten."

Her disbelief lasted only moments before mischief and excitement replaced it. "You're on."

Nine

"It's…good to hear your voice, Father."

Kanza hated that hesitation in her voice. Whatever her father's faults, she did love him. Did miss him.

Yeah. She did. But, and it was a huge but, after ten minutes of basking in the nostalgia of early and oblivious childhood when her father had been her hero, she always thudded back to reality and was ready not to see him again for months.

"It's great to hear yours, *ya bnayti.*"

His calling her *my daughter,* instead of bestowing a personalized greeting with her name included, annoyed her. He called his other eight daughters that, with the same indiscrimination. She thought he used it most times because he forgot the name of the one he was talking to.

Curbing her irritation, and knowing her father never called unless he had something to ask of her, she said, "Anything I can do for you, Father?"

"*Ya Ullah,* yes. Only you can help me now, *ya bnayti.* I need you to come back to Zohayd at once."

Ten minutes later, she sat staring numbly into space. She'd tried to wriggle out of saying yes. She'd failed.

She was really going back to Zohayd. Tonight.

Her father had begged her to board the first flight to Zohayd. Beyond confirming that no one was dead or severely injured, he'd said no more about why he needed her back so urgently.

She reserved a ticket online, then packed a few essentials. She wouldn't stay a minute longer than necessary.

Not that there was a reason to hurry back.

Not from the evidence of the past two weeks anyway.

It had been then, six weeks after that magical time in Aram's new apartment and the breakfast in Barbados, that Aram had suddenly become insanely busy. He'd neglected his work so much that the accumulation had become critical.

She understood. Of *course,* she did. She knew exactly how many people depended on him, what kind of money rode on his presence and expertise. She'd been neglecting her work, too, but Johara had picked up the slack, and she was not so indispensable that her absence would cause the same widespread ripples his had. She appreciated this fully. Mentally. But otherwise…

The fact was, he'd spoiled her. She'd gotten reliant on seeing him each and every day, on being able to pick up the phone, day or night, and he'd be eager and willing to grant her every wish, to be there with her at no notice. When that had suddenly come to an abrupt end, she'd gone into withdrawal.

God. She'd turned into one of those clingy, needy females. At least in her own mind and psyche. Outwardly, she was her devil-may-care self. At least, she hoped she was.

But she was something else, too. Moronic. The man had a life outside her, even if for three months straight it had seemed as if he didn't. She'd known real life would reassert itself at one point. So she should stop whining *now.*

And now that she thought of it without self-pity, going to Zohayd was a good thing. She'd been twiddling her thumbs until she and Johara started the next project. And by the time she was back, he would have sorted himself enough to be able to see her again—at least more than he had the past two weeks.

She speed-dialed his number. The voice she now lived to hear poured into her brain after the second ring.

"Kanza—a moment please…" His voice was muffled as he talked to someone.

Feeling guilty for interrupting him when he'd told her he wouldn't have a free moment before seven, she rushed on. "I just wanted to tell you I'm going home in a couple of hours."

More muffled words, then he came back to her. "That's fantastic. About time."

That she hadn't expected. "It—it is?"

"Sure, it is. Listen, Kanza, I'm sorry, but I *have* to finish this before the Saudi Stock Exchange opens. 'Bye now."

Then he hung up.

She stared at the phone.

Last night, he'd said he'd see her later tonight. But she'd just told him she wouldn't be able to see him because she was traveling and he'd sounded…glad?

Had she unwittingly let her disappointment show when he'd been unable to see her for the past two weeks, and he now thought it was a good idea if she did something other than wait for him until his preoccupation lightened and he could see her again?

But he hadn't even asked why she was going or how long she'd stay. Sure, he'd been in a hurry, but he could have said something other than *fantastic* or *about time*. He could have said he'd call later to get details.

So was it possible he was just glad to get her off his back? Could it be that what she'd thought were unfounded feelings of impending loss had just been premonition? Was the magical interlude with him really over?

She'd known from the start he'd just needed someone to help him through the worst slump in his life. Now that he was over it, was he over his need for her?

That made sense. Terrible sense. And it was only expected. She'd dreaded that day, but she'd known it would
come. She'd just kept hoping it would not come so soon.
She wasn't ready to give him up yet.

But when would she ever be? How could she ever be…
when she loved him?

Suddenly a sob tore out of her. Then another, and another
until she was bent over, tears raining on the ground, unable
to contain the torrent of anguish anymore.

She loved him.

She would forever love him.

And she would have remained his friend forever, asking
nothing more but to have the pleasure and privilege of his
nearness, of his appreciation, of his completion. Of his need.

But it seemed he no longer needed her.

Now he'd recede, but never really end it as he would have
with a lover. She would see him again and again whenever
life threw them together. And each time, he'd expect her to
be his buddy, would chat and tease and reminisce and not
realize that she missed him like an amputee would a limb.

Maybe going to Zohayd now *was* a blessing in disguise.

Maybe she should stay until he totally forgot about her.

The moment Aram finished his last memo for the night,
he pounced on his phone to call Kanza. Before he did, Shaheen walked into his office.

A groan escaped him that he had to postpone the call—
and seeing her—for the length of Shaheen's visit.

His brother-in-law whistled. "*Ya Ullah,* you missed me
that much?"

Aram winced. His impatience must be emblazoned
across his whole body. And he'd been totally neglecting
his friend as of late. But he'd been reserving every hour,
every moment, every spare breath for Kanza.

"Actually I do miss you, but—" he groaned again, ran
his fingers through his hair "—you know how it is."

Shaheen laughed. *"Menn la'ah ahbaboh nessi ashaboh."* *He who finds his loved ones forgets his friends.*

He refused to comment on Shaheen's backhanded reference to Kanza as his loved one. "As much as I'd love to indulge your curiosity, Shaheen, I have to go to Kanza now. Let's get together some other time. Maybe I'll bring Kanza over to your home, hmm?"

Shaheen blinked in surprise. "You're going to Zohayd?"

Aram scowled. "Now, where did that come from? Why should I go to Zohayd?"

"Because you said that you're going to Kanza, who's on her way to Zohayd right now."

Aram glanced at his watch, then out of the jet's window, then back at his watch.

Had it always taken that long to get to Zohayd?

It felt as if it had been a day since he'd boarded his jet—barely an hour after Shaheen had said Kanza was heading there.

He was still reverberating with disbelief. With…panic.

His condition had been worsening since it had sunk in that the "home" Kanza had meant was Zohayd. According to Johara, Kanza was returning there at her father's urgent demand. Kanza herself didn't know why. Shaheen hadn't been able to understand why he'd be so agitated that she was visiting her family and would probably be back in a few days.

But he'd been unable to listen, to Shaheen or the voice of reason. Nothing had mattered but one thing.

The need to go after her.

A tornado was tearing through him. His gut told him something was wrong. Terribly wrong.

For how could she go like that without saying goodbye?

Even if she had to rush, even if he'd been swamped, the Kanza he knew would have let him see her before separation was imposed on them.

So why hadn't she? Why hadn't she made it clear where she was going? If he'd known, he would have rushed to her, would have paid the millions that would have been lost for a chance to see her even for a few minutes before she left. She had to know he would have. So why hadn't she given him the chance to? Hadn't it been as necessary for her to see him this last time as it was for him?

Was he not as necessary to her as she was to him?

He'd long been forced to believe his necessity to her differed from hers to him. He'd thought that as long as the intimacy remained the same, he'd just have to live with the fact that its…texture wasn't what he now yearned for.

But what if he was losing even that? What if not saying goodbye now meant that she *could* eventually say goodbye for real? What if that day was even closer than his worst nightmares?

What if that day was here?

He couldn't even face that possibility. He'd lost his solitariness from the first time he'd seen her. She'd proceeded to strip him of his self-containment, his autonomy. He'd known isolation. But he hadn't realized what loneliness was until he'd heard from Shaheen that she'd left.

She'd become more than vital to him. She'd become… home.

What if he could never be anything like that to her?

What if he caught up with her in Zohayd and she only thought he was out of his mind hurtling after her like that?

Maybe he was out of his mind. Maybe everything he'd just churned himself over had no basis in fact. Maybe…

His cell phone rang. He fumbled with it, his fingers going numb with brutal anticipation. *Kanza.* She'd tell him why she hadn't said goodbye. And he'd tell her he'd be with her in a couple of hours and she could say it to his face.

The next moment disappointment crashed through him. Johara.

He couldn't hold back his growl. "What is it, Johara?"

A silent beat. "Uh...don't kill the messenger, okay?"

"What the hell does that mean? Jo, I'm really not in any condition to have a nice, civil conversation right now. For both our sakes, just leave me alone."

"I'm sorry, Aram, but I really think you need to know, so you'd be prepared."

"Know what? Be prepared for what?" A thousand dreads swooped down on him, each one shrieking Kanza, Kanza, *Kanza*... "Just spit it out!"

"I just got off the phone with Kanza's father. He said he needed me to know as Kanza's best friend that Prince Kareem Aal Kahlawi has asked for her hand in marriage."

Kanza thought it was inevitable.

She would end up killing someone.

For now, storming through her father's house, slamming her old bedroom door behind her was all the venting she could do.

She leaned against it, letting out a furious shriek.

Of all the self-involved, self-serving, unfeeling... Argh!

To think that was why her father had dragged her back here!

Couldn't she kill him? And her sisters? Just a little bit...?

Her whole body lurched forward, every nerve firing at once.

She stopped. Moving. Breathing. Even her heart slowed down. Each boom so hard her ears rang.

That must be it. Why she thought she'd heard...

"Kanza."

Aram.

God. She was starting to hear things. Hear him. When he was seven thousand miles away. This was beyond pathetic....

"Kanza. I know you're there."

Okay. She wasn't *that* pathetic.

"I saw you tearing out of the living room, saw you going

up. I know this is your room. I know you're in there now. Come to the window. *Now,* Kanza."

That last "now" catapulted her to the French doors. She barely stopped before she shot over the balcony's balustrade.

And standing down there, among the shrubs below, in all his mind-blowing glory, was Aram.

Azure bolts arced from his eyes and a wounded lion's growl came from his lips. "What are you *doing* here?"

Her head spun at the brunt of his beauty under Zohayd's declining sun and the absurdity of his question.

She blinked, as if it would reboot her brain. "What are *you* doing here? In Zohayd? And standing beneath my window?"

He stuck his fists at his hips. He looked…angry? And agitated. Why? "What does it look like? I'm here to see you."

She shook her head, confusion deepening. He must have left New York just a few hours after she had. Had he come all the way here to find out why she had? After he'd basically told her to scram? Why not just call? What did it all mean?

Okay. With the upheaval of this past day, her brain was on the fritz. She could no longer attempt to make any sense of it.

She pinched the bridge of her nose. "Well, you saw me. Now go away before all my family comes out and finds you here. With the way you've been shouting, they must be on their way."

He widened his stance, face adamant planes and ruthless slashes. "If you don't want them to see me, come down."

"I can't. If I go down and try to walk through the front door, I'll have twenty females on my case…and I don't want the ulcer I've acquired in the last hours to rupture."

"Then *climb* down."

That last whisper could have sandpapered the manor's facade. "Okay, Aram, I know you're crazy, but even in your insanity you can see that the last foothold is twenty feet above splat level."

He shrugged. "Fifteen max. I'll catch you."

Closing her mouth before it caught one of the birds zooming back to their nests at the approach of sunset, she echoed his pose, fists on hips. "If you want to reenact Shaheen's stunt with Johara, I have to remind you that she was six at the time."

That shrug again. "You're not that much bigger now."

She coughed a chagrined laugh. "Why, thanks. Just what every grown woman wants to hear."

He sighed. "I meant the ratio of your size to mine, compared to that of fourteen-year-old Shaheen to six-year-old Johara." He suddenly snarled again, his eyes blazing. "Stop arguing. I can catch you, easy. You know I've been exercising."

Yeah, she knew. She'd attended many a mind-scrambling session, seen what he looked like with minimal clothing, flexing, bulging, sweating, flooding a mile's radius with premium, lethal testosterone.

"But even in my worst days, I would have been able to catch you. I always knew I was that big for a reason, but I just never knew what it was. Now I know. It's so I could catch you."

Her mouth dropped open again.

What that man kept *saying*.

What would he say when he was actually in love…?

That thought made her feel like jumping off the balcony—and not so he could catch her.

She inhaled a steadying, sanity-laced breath. "Oh, all right. Just because I know you'll stand there until I do. Or worse, barge into the house to come up here and have a houseful of your old fans pick your bones. I hope you know I'm doing this to save your gorgeous hide."

His smile was terse. "Yes, of course. I'm, as always, eternally indebted to you. Now hurry."

Mumbling under her breath about him being a hulk-sized brat who expected to get his way in everything, she took one last bracing breath and climbed over the balustrade.

As she inched down over the steplike ledges, he kept a running encouragement. "You're doing fine. Don't look down. I'm right here."

Slipping, she clung to the building, wailed, "Shut *up,* Aram. God, I can't believe what you can talk me into."

He just kept going. "Keep your body firm, not tense, okay? Now let go." When she hesitated, his voice suddenly dropped into the darkest reaches of hypnosis. "Don't worry, I'll catch you, *ya kanzi.*"

My treasure.

All her nerves unraveled. She plummeted.

Her plunge came to a jarring, if firm and secure, end.

He'd caught her. Easy, as he'd said. As if he'd snatched her from a three-foot drop. And she was staring up into those vivid, luminescent eyes that now filled her existence.

Without one more word, he swept her along through the manicured grounds and out of her father's estate.

She reeled. Not from the drop, but from her first contact with him. His flesh pressed to hers, his warmth enveloping her, his strength cocooning her. Being in his arms, even if in this context, was like…like…going home.

Even if the feeling was imaginary, she'd savor it. He was here, for whatever reason, and their…closeness wasn't over.

Not yet.

She let go, let him take her wherever he would.

Aram brooded at Kanza as she walked one step ahead.

He could barely let her be this far away. He'd clutched her all the way out of her father's estate, almost unable to let her go to put her into the car. As if by agreement, they hadn't said anything during the drive. But it hadn't been the companionable silence they'd perfected. By the time they'd arrived, he'd expended his decimated willpower so he wouldn't roar, demanding she tell him what was wrong.

She turned every few steps, as if to check if he was maintaining the same distance. Her glances felt like the sustenance that would save him from starvation. But they didn't soothe him as they'd always done. There was something in them that sent his senses haywire. Something…wary.

He couldn't bear to interpret this. Any interpretation was just too mutilating. And could be dead wrong anyway. So he wouldn't even try.

She stopped at the railings of the upper-floor terrace, turning to him. "Don't tell me you bought this villa in your half hour in Zohayd before popping up beneath my window."

He barely caught back a groan of relief. Her voice. Her teasing. God, he *needed* them.

"Why? Do you think I'm not crazy enough to do it?"

Her smile resembled her usual ones. But not quite. "Excellent point. Since you're crazier, you might have also bought the sea and desert in a ten-mile radius."

A laugh caught in his throat, broke against the spastic barrier of tension. "It's Shaheen's. Now tell me what the hell you're doing here. And why you left without telling me."

Her eyes got even more enormous. "I did tell you."

He threw his arms wide in frustration. "How was I supposed to know you meant Zohayd when you said home?"

"Uh…is this a new crisis? What else could I have meant?"

"Your old New York apartment, of course. The one you said felt like home, the one I got you back the lease for. I thought you were finally ready to move there again."

"That's why you thought it fantastic when I said I was going home," she said, as if to herself. "You thought it was about time I was down the street from you."

He gaped at her. "Are you *nuts?* You thought I would *actually* think it fantastic for you to come out here and leave me alone in New York? Contrary to popular belief, I'm not that evolved. I might support your doing something that doesn't involve me if it makes you happy, even accept that it could take you away from me—for a little while—but be okay, let alone ecstatic about it? No way."

Her eyes kept widening with his every word. At his last bark, her smile flashed back to its unbridled vivacity.

"Thanks for letting me know the extent of your evolution. Now quit snarling at me. I have a big enough headache being saddled with making decisions for more than you now, in not only one but *two* weddings."

It felt as if a missile had hit him.

No. She couldn't be talking about a wedding already. He couldn't allow it. He wouldn't. He'd…

Two weddings?

His rumble was that of a beast bewildered with too many blows. "What the hell are you talking about?"

"My last two unmarried sisters' weddings. With each from a different mother and with how things are in Zohayd where weddings are battlefields, they've reached a standoff with each other and with their bridegrooms' families. It seems there's more hope of ending a war than reaching an agreement on the details of the weddings. Enter me—what Father thinks is his only hope of defusing the situation."

He frowned. "Why you?"

Her lips twisted whimsically. "Because I'm what Father calls the 'neutral zone.' With me as the one daughter of the woman who gave birth to me then ran off with a big chunk of my father's wealth, I am the one who has always given him no trouble, having no mother to harass him on my behalf. And being stuck as the middle sister between eight half sisters, four each from a stepmother, it made me the one in his brood of nine female offspring that no one is jealous of, therefore not unreasonably contentious with." She sighed dramatically. "I was always dragged to referee, because both sides don't consider me a player in the family power games at all. Now Father has recruited me to get all these hysterical females off his back and hopefully get those weddings under way and over with."

What about the groom who proposed to you? That... prince? *Why aren't you telling me about him?*

The questions backlashed in his chest. He couldn't give this preposterous subject credence by even mentioning it.

There was only one thing to ask now.

"Is it me?"

She stared up at him, standing against the winter sunset's backdrop, its fire reflecting gold on her skin and striking flames from the depths of her onyx eyes and the thick mahogany satin tresses that undulated around her in the breeze. She was the embodiment of his every taste and desire and aspiration. And the picture of incomprehension.

But he could no longer afford the luxury of caution. Not when he had the grenade of that...*prince's*...proposal lying there between them. Not when letting the status quo continue could give it a chance to explode and cost him everything.

He halved the step he'd been keeping between them. "You're the only one who's ever told me the whole truth, Kanza. I need you to give it to me now."

Her gaze flickered, but she only nodded. She would give him that truth. Always.

And that truth might end his world.

But he had to have it. "I believe in pure friendship between a man and a woman. But when they share... everything, I can't see how there'd be no physical attraction at all. So, again, is it me? Or are you generally not interested?"

No total truth came from her. Just total astonishment.

He groaned. "It's clear this has never even crossed your mind. And I've been content with what we share, delighted our friendship is rooted in intellectual and spiritual harmony—and I was willing to wait forever for anything else. But I feel I don't have forever anymore. And I can't live with the idea that maybe you just aren't aware of the possibilities, that if I can persuade you to give it a try, you might…not hate it."

Still nothing. Nothing but gaping.

And he put his worst fear into words. "Were you stating your personal preferences that first night? When you said I was disgustingly pretty? Do your tastes run toward something, I don't know, rougher or softer or just not…this?" He made a tense gesture at his face, his body. "Do you have an ideal of masculinity and I'm just not it?"

Her cheeks and lips were now hectic rose. Her voice wavered. "Uh… I'm really not sure…"

Neither was he. If it would be even adequate between them. If he could even please her.

But he felt everything for her, wanted everything with her, so he had to try.

He reached for her, cupped her precious head and gazed down into her shocked eyes. "There's one way to make sure."

Then he swooped down and took her lips.

At the first contact with her flesh, the first flay of her breath, a thousand volts crackled between them, unleashing everything inside him in a tidal wave.

Lashed by the ferocity of his response and immediacy of her surrender, he captured her dainty lower lip in a growling bite, stilling its tremors, attempting to moderate his greed. She only cried out, arched against him and opened her lips wider. And her taste inundated him.

God…her *taste*. He'd imagined but couldn't have possibly anticipated her unimaginable sweetness. Or the perfume of her breath or the sensory overload of her feel. Or what it would all do to him. Everything about her mixed in an aphrodisiac, a hallucinogen that eddied in his arteries and pounded through his system, snapping the tethers of his sanity.

He could have held back from acting on his insanity, could have moderated his onslaught if not for the way she melted against him, blasting away all doubts about her capacity for passion in the inferno of her response. Her moans and whimpers urged him on to take his possession from tasting to clinging to wrenching.

His hands shook with urgency as he gathered her thighs, opened her around his bulk, pinned her against the railings with the force of his hunger. Plundering her with his tongue, he drove inside her mouth, thrust against her heat, losing rhythm in the wildness, losing his mind.

But even without a mind or will, his love for this irreplaceable being was far more potent than even his will to live. She did mean more than life to him.

Tearing out of their merging, rumbling at the sting of separation, he looked down at the overpowering sight of the woman trembling in his arms. "Do you want this, Kanza? Do you want *me?*"

Her dark eyes scorched him with what he'd never dreamed of seeing in them: drugged sensuality and surrender. Then they squeezed in languorous acquiescence.

He needed more. A full disclosure, a knowing consent.

"I will take everything you have, devour everything you are, give you all of me. Do you understand? Is this what you want? What you need? *Everything* with me, now?"

His heart faltered, afraid to beat, waiting for her verdict. Then its valves almost burst as her parted, passion-swollen lips quivered on a ragged, drawn-out sigh.

A simple, devastating, "Yes."

Ten

Kanza heard herself moaning "yes" to Aram as if from the depths of a dream. What *had* to be a dream.

For how could this be reality? How could she be in Aram's arms? How could it be that he'd been devouring her and was now asking for more, for everything?

The only reason she believed it was real was that no dream could be this intense, this incredible. And because no dream of hers about him had been anything like this.

In her wildest fantasies, Aram, her indulgent friend, had been gentle in his approach, tender in his passion.

But the Aram she'd known was gone. In his place was a marauder: wild, almost rough and barely holding back to make certain she wanted his invasion and sanctioned his ferocity.

And she did. Oh, how she did. She'd said yes. Couldn't have said more. She could barely hold on to consciousness as she found herself swept up in the throes of his unexpected, shocking passion. The thrill of his dominance, the starkness of his lust tampered with everything that powered her, body and being. Her brain waves blipped, her heartbeat plunged into arrhythmia, her every cell swelled, throbbed, screamed for his possession and assuagement.

She'd thought she'd been aroused around him. Now she knew what arousal was. This mindlessness, this avalanche of sensations, this need to be conquered, dominated, ravished. By him, only him.

Almost swooning with the force of need, she delighted in openly devouring him, indulging her greed for his splendor. He loomed above her, the fiery palette of the horizon framing his bulk, accentuating his size, setting his beauty ablaze. The tempest in his eyes was precariously checked. He was giving her one last chance to recant her surrender. Before he devastated her.

She would die if he didn't.

The only confirmation she was capable of was to melt back into his embrace, arching against him in fuller surrender.

Growling something under his breath, he bent toward her. Thinking he'd scoop her up into his arms, carry her inside and take full possession of her, she felt shock reverberate when he started undoing her shirt. He planned to make love to her out here!

There was no one around in what looked like a hundred-mile radius, but she still squirmed. One arm firmed around her only enough to still her as his other hand drifted up her body and behind her to unclasp her bra. The relief of pressure on her swollen flesh buckled her legs.

He held her up, his eyes roving her body in fierce greed as he rid her of her jacket, shirt and bra. The moment her breasts spilled out, he bared his teeth, his lips emitting a soft snarl of hunger. Before she could beg for those lips and teeth on her, his hand undid her pants. She gaped as he dropped to his knees, spanning her hips in his hands' girdle of fire; his fingers hooked into both pants and panties and swept both off her, along with her shoes.

Suddenly his hands reversed their path, inflaming her flesh, rendering her breathless, and he stilled an inch from her core.

She shook—and not with cold. If it wasn't for the cooling air, she might have spontaneously combusted.

Then he lit her fuse, raising eyes like incendiary precious stones. *"Ma koll hada'l jamaal? Kaif konti tekhfeeh?"*

Hearing him raggedly speaking Arabic, asking how she had hidden all this beauty, made her writhe. "Aram... please..."

"Aih...I'll please you, *ya kanzi.*" His face pressed to her thighs, her abdomen, his lips opening over her quivering flesh, sucking, nibbling everywhere like a starving man who didn't know where to start his feast. Her fingers convulsed in his silky hair, pressed his face to her flesh in an ecstasy of torment, unable to bear the stimulation, unable to get enough. He took her breasts in hands that trembled, pressed them, cradled them, kneaded and nuzzled them as if they were the most amazing things he'd ever felt. Tears broke through her fugue of arousal. "Please, Aram..."

He closed his eyes as if in pain and buried his face in her breasts, inhaling her, opening his mouth over her taut flesh, testing and tasting, lavishing her with his teeth and tongue. *"Sehr, jonoon, ehsasek, reehtek, taamek..."*

Magic, madness, your feel, your scent, your taste...

Her mind unraveled with every squeeze, each rub and nip and probe, each with the exact force, the exact roughness to extract maximum pleasure from her every nerve ending. He layered sensation with each press and bite until she felt devoured, set aflame. Something inside her was charring.

Her undulations against him became feverish, her clamoring flesh seeking any part of him in mindless pursuit of relief. Her begging became a litany until he dragged an electric hand between her thighs, tormenting his way to her core. The heel of his thumb delved between her outer lips at the same moment the damp furnace of his mouth finally clamped over one of the nipples that screamed for his possession. Sensations slashed her nerves.

Supporting her collapsing weight with an arm around

her hips, he slid two fingers between her molten inner lips, stilling at her entrance. "I didn't think that I'd ever see you like this, open for me, on fire, hunger shaking you apart, that I would be able to pleasure you like this…."

He spread her legs, placed one after the other over his shoulders, opening her core for his pleasure and possession. Her moans now merged into an incessant sound of suffering.

He inhaled her again, rumbling like a lion maddened at the scent of his female in heat, as she was. Then he blew a gust of acute sensation over the knot where her nerves converged. She bucked, her plea choking. It became a shriek when he pumped a finger inside her in a slow, slow glide. Sunset turned to darkest night as she convulsed, pleasure slamming through her in desperate surges.

Her sight burst back to an image from a fantasy. Aram, fully clothed, kneeling between her legs…her, naked, splayed open over his shoulders, amidst an empty planet all their own.

And he'd made her climax with one touch.

Among the mass of aftershocks, she felt his finger, still inside her, pumping…beckoning. Her gasp tore through her lungs as his tongue joined in, licked from where his finger was buried inside her upward, circling her bud. Each glide and graze and pull and thrust sent hotter lances skewering through her as if she hadn't just had the most intense orgasm of her life. It was only when she sobbed, bucked, pressed her burning flesh to his mouth, opening herself fully to his double assault, that his lips locked on her core and really gave it to her, had her quaking and screaming with an even more violent release.

She tumbled from the explosive peak, drained, sated. Stupefied. What had just happened?

Her drugged eyes sought his, as if for answers.

Even in the receding sunset they glowed azure, heavy with hunger and satisfaction. "You better have really en-

joyed this, because I'm now addicted to your taste and pleasure."

Something tightened inside her until it became almost
painful. She was flabbergasted to recognize it as an even
fiercer arousal. Her satisfaction had lasted only a minute,
and now she was even hungrier. No. Something else she'd
never felt before. Empty. As if there was a gnawing void inside her that demanded to be filled. By him. Only ever him.

She confessed it all to him. "The pleasure you gave me
is nothing like I ever imagined. But I hope you're not thinking of indulging your addiction again. I want pleasure *with*
you."

All lightness drained from his eyes as he reached for
her again. He cupped her, then squeezed her mound pos-
sessively, desensitizing her, the ferocious conqueror flaring
back to life. "And you will have it. I'll ride you to ecstasy
until you can't beg for more."

Her senses swam with the force of anticipation, with the
searing delight of his sensual threat. Her heart went haywire
as he swept her up in his arms and headed inside.

In minutes, he entered a huge, tastefully furnished suite
with marble floors, Persian carpets and soaring ceilings.
At the thought that it must be Johara and Shaheen's master
suite, a flush engulfed her body.

A gigantic circular bed draped in chocolate satin spread
beneath a domed skylight that glowed with the last tendrils
of sunset. Oil lamps blazed everywhere, swathing everything in a golden cast of mystery and intimacy.

Sinking deeper into sensory overload, she tried to drag
him down on top of her as he set her on the bed. He sowed
kisses over her face and clinging arms as he withdrew, then
stood back looking down at her.

His breath shuddered out. "Do you realize how incredible you are?" Elation, embarrassment, but mainly disbelief
gurgled in her throat. "Do you want to *see* how incredible
I find you?"

That got her voice working. "Yes, *please*."

She struggled up to her elbows as he started to strip, exposing each sculpted inch, showing her how incredible *he* was. Her eyes and mouth watered, her hands stung with the intensity of need to explore him, revel in him. He did have the body of a higher being. It was a miracle he wore clothes at all, didn't go through life flaunting his perfection and driving poor inferior mortals crazy with lust and envy.

Then he stepped out of his boxers, released the...proof of how incredible he found her, and a spike of craving and intimidation had her collapsing onto her back.

She'd felt he was big when he'd pressed against her what felt like a lifetime ago back on the terrace. But this... What if she couldn't accommodate him, couldn't please him?

But she had to give him everything, had to take all he had. Her heart would stop beating if he didn't make her his now. *Now.*

His muscles bunched with barely suppressed desire as he came down onto the bed, his hunger crashing over her in drowning waves. "No more waiting, *ya kanzi*. Now I take you. And you take me."

"Yes." She held out shaking arms as he surged over her, impacted her. She cried out, reveling in how her softness cushioned his hardness. Perfect. No, sublime.

He dragged her legs apart even as she opened them for him. He guided them around his waist, his eyes seeking hers, solicitous and tempestuous, his erection seeking her entrance. Finding it both hot and molten, he bathed himself in her flowing readiness in one teasing stroke from her bud to her opening.

On the next stroke, he growled his surrender, sank inside her, fierce and full.

The world detonated in a crimson flash and then disappeared.

In the darkness, she heard keening as if from the end of

a tunnel, and everything was shuddering. Then she went nerveless, collapsed beneath him in profound sensual shock.

She didn't know how long existence was condensed into the exquisite agony. Then the world surged back on her with a flood of sensations, none she'd ever felt before.

She found him turned to stone on top of her, face and body, eyes wild with worry. "It's your first time."

As she quivered inside and out, a laugh burst out, startling them both. "As if this is a surprise. Have you met me?"

The consternation gripping his face vanished and was replaced by sensuality and tenderness. "Oh, yes, I have. And oh, yes, it is—*you* are a surprise a second."

He started withdrawing from her depths.

The emptiness he left behind made her feel as if she'd implode. "No, don't go…don't stop…."

Throwing his head back, he squeezed his eyes. "I'm going nowhere. In consideration of your mint condition, I'm just trying to adjust from the fast and furious first time I had in mind to something that's slower and more leisurely…." He opened his eyes and gazed down at her. "I would only stop if you wanted me to."

Feeling the emptiness inside her threatening to engulf her, she thrust her hips upward, uncaring about the burning, even needing it. "I'd die if you stop."

His groan was as pained, as if she'd hurt him, too. "Stopping would probably finish me, as well. For real."

She thrust up again, crying out at the razing sensations as he stretched her beyond her limits. "You'd still stop… if I asked?"

A hand stabbed through her hair, dragged her down by its tether to the mattress, pinning her there for his ferocious proclamation. "I'd die if you asked."

Her heart gave a thunderclap inside her chest, shaking her like an earthquake. Tears she'd long repressed rose and poured from her very depths.

She surged up, clung to him, crushed herself against his

steel-fleshed body. "*Ya Ullah, ya* Aram, I'd die for you, too. Take me, leave no part of me, finish me. Don't hold back, hurt me until you make it better...."

"*Aih, ya kanzi,* I'll make it better. I'll make it so much better...." He cupped her hips in both hands, tilted them into a fully surrendering cradle for his then ever so slowly thrust himself to the hilt inside her.

It was beyond overwhelming, being occupied by him, being full of him. The reality of it, the sheer meaning and carnality of it, rocked her to the core. She collapsed, buried under the sensations.

He withdrew again, and she cried out at the unbearable loss, urged him to sink back into her. He resisted her writhing pleas, his shaft resting at her entrance before he plunged inside her again. She cried out a hot gust of passion, opening wider for him.

He kept her gaze prisoner as he watched her, gauging her reactions, adjusting his movements to her every gasp and moan and grimace, waiting for pleasure to submerge the pain. He kept her at a fever pitch, caressing her all over, suckling her breasts, draining her lips, raining wonder over her.

Then her body poured new readiness and pleasure over him, and he bent to drive his tongue inside her to his plunging rhythm, quickening both, until she felt a storm gathering inside her, felt she'd shatter if it broke.

His groan reverberated inside her mouth. "Perfection, *ya kanzi,* inside and out. Everything about you, with you."

Everything inside her tightened unbearably, her depths rippling around him, reaching for that elusive something that she felt she'd perish if she didn't have it, now, now.

She cried out, "Please, Aram, please, give it to me now, everything, *everything*...."

And he obliged her. Tilting her toward him, angling his thrusts, he drove into her with the exact force and speed she needed until he did it, shattered the coil of tension.

She heaved up beneath him so hard she raised them both in the air before crashing back to the bed. Convulsion after convulsion tore through her, clamped her around him. Her insides splintered on pleasure too sharp to register at first, then to bear, then to bear having it end.

Then she felt it, the moment his body caught the current of her desperation, a moment she'd replay in her memory forever. The sight and feel of him as he surrendered inside her to the ecstasy the searing sweetness of their union had brought him.

She peaked again as he threw his head back to roar his pleasure, feeding her convulsions with his own, pouring his release on her conflagration, jetting it inside her in hot surges until she felt completely and utterly filled.

Nothingness consumed her. For a moment, or an hour. Then she was surging back into her body, shaking, weeping, aftershocks demolishing what was left of her.

He *had* finished her, as she'd begged him to.

Then he was moving, and panic surged. She clung to him, unable to be apart from him now. He pressed soothing kisses to her swollen eyes, murmuring reassurance in that voice that strummed everything in her as he swept her around, took her over him, careful not to jar her, ensuring he remained inside her.

Then she was lying on top of him, the biggest part of her soul, satiated in ways she couldn't have imagined, at once reverberating with the enormity of the experience, and in perfect peace for the first time in her life.

She lay there merged with him, fused to him, awe overtaking her at everything that had happened.

Then her heart stopped thundering enough to let her breathe properly, to raise her head, to access her voice.

She heard herself asking, "What—what was…that?"

He stared up at her, his eyes just as dazed, his lips twitching into a smile. "I…have absolutely no idea. So *that* was sex, huh?"

"Hey…that's my line."

"Then you'll have to share it with me."

He withdrew from her depths carefully, making her realize that his erection hadn't subsided. His groan echoed her moan at the burn of separation. He soothed her, suckling her nipples until she wrapped herself around him again.

Unclasping her thighs from around him, he gave a distressed laugh. "You might think you're ready for another round of devastation, but trust me, you're not." He propped himself on his elbow, gathered her along his length, looking down at her with such sensual indulgence, her core flowed again. "It's merciful I had no idea it would be like this between us or I would have pounced on you long ago."

Feeling free and incredibly wanton, she rubbed her hands down his chest and twined her legs through his. "You should have."

He pressed into her, daunting arousal undiminished, body buzzing with vitality and dominance and lust. "I should make you pay for all these times you looked at me as if I was the brother you never had."

She arched, opening for his erection, needing him back inside her. "You should."

He chuckled, a dozen devils dancing in his incredible eyes. "Behave. You're too sore now. Give it an hour or two, then I'll…make you pay."

"Make me pay now. I loved the way you made me sore so much I almost died of pleasure. Make me sore again, Aram."

"And all this time I was afraid you were this sexless tomboy. Then after one kiss, that disguise you wear comes off and there's the most perfectly formed and uninhibited sex goddess beneath it all. You almost did kill me with pleasure, too."

"How about we flirt with mortal danger some more?"

"Sahrah."

Calling her *enchantress,* he crushed her in his arms and

thrust against her, sliding his erection up and down between the lips of her core, nudging her nub over and over.

The pleasure was unimaginable, built so quickly, a sweet, sharp burn in her blood, a tightening in her depths that now knew exactly how to unfurl and undo her. She opened herself wide for him, let him pleasure her this way.

Feeling the advance tremors of a magnificent orgasm strengthening, she undulated faster against him. Her pleas became shrieks as pleasure tore through her.

He pinned her beneath him as she thrashed, bucked, gliding over his hardness to the exact pressure and rhythm to drain her of the last spark of pleasure her body needed to discharge.

Then, kneeling between her splayed legs, he pumped his erection a few last times and roared as he climaxed over her.

She'd never seen anything as incredible, as fulfilling as watching him take his pleasure, rain it over the body he'd just owned and pleasured. The sight of his face in the grip of orgasm...

Then he was coming down half over her, mingling the beats of their booming hearts.

"Now I might have a heart attack thinking of all the times I was hard as steel around you and didn't realize this—" he made an explicit gesture at all of her spread beneath him, no doubt the very sight of abandon "—was in store for me if I just grabbed you and plunged inside you."

"Sorry for wasting your time being so oblivious."

His eyes were suddenly anxious, fervent. "You wasted nothing. I was just joking. I can never describe how grateful I am that we became friends first. I wouldn't change a second we had together, *ya kanzi*. Say you believe that."

She brought him down to her. "I believe *you*. Always. And I feel exactly the same. I wouldn't change a thing."

She didn't know anything more but that she was surrounded by passion and protection and sinking into a realm of absolute safety and contentment....

* * *

She woke up to the best sight on the planet.

A naked Aram standing at the window, gazing outside through a crack in the shutters. From the spear of light, she judged it must be almost sunset again. He'd woken her up twice through the night and day, showed her again and again that there was no limit to the pleasure they could share.

As if feeling her eyes on him, he turned at once, his smile the best dawn she'd ever witnessed.

She struggled to sit up in bed as he brought her a tray. Then he sat beside her, feeding her, cossetting her. The blatant intimacy in his eyes suddenly made her blush as everything they'd done together washed over her. She buried her flaming face in his chest.

He laughed out loud. "You're just unbearably cute being shy now after you blew my mind and every cell in my body with how responsive and uninhibited you are."

"It's a side effect of being transfigured, being a first timer," she mumbled against the velvet overlying steel of his skin and flesh.

"I was a first timer, too." She frowned up at him. "I *was* as untried as you in what passion—towering, consuming, earth-shattering passion—was like. So the experience was just as transformative for me as it was for you."

Joy overwhelmed her, had her burrowing deeper in his chest. "I'll take your word for it."

He chuckled, raised her face. "Now I want to take *your* word. That you won't do what your sisters did."

"What do you mean?"

"That you won't ask for a million contradictory details. That you won't do a thing to postpone our wedding."

Eleven

"What do you mean *wedding?*"

Aram's smile widened as Kanza sprang up, sitting like the cat she reminded him of, switching from bone-deep relaxation to full-on alertness in a heartbeat. Everything inside him knotted and hardened again as his gaze roved down that body that had taught him the meaning of "almost died of pleasure."

He reached an aching hand to cup that breast that filled it as if it was made to its measurement. "I mean our wedding."

"Our…" Her face scrunched as if with pain. "Stop it right this second, okay? Just…don't. *Don't,* Aram."

His heart contracted so hard it hurt. "Don't what?"

"Don't start with 'doing the right thing.'"

He frowned. "What the hell do you mean by that?"

She rose to her knees to scowl down at him. "I mean you think you've seduced a 'virgin,' had unprotected sex with her a handful of times and probably put a kid inside her by now. Having long been infected with Zohaydan conservatism, you think it's unquestionable that you have to marry me."

He rose to his knees, too, towering over her, needing to

overwhelm her and her faulty assumptions before this got any further. "If there is a kid in there, I'd want with every fiber of my being to be its father…."

"And that's no reason to get married."

He pressed on. "And to be the best friend, lover and husband of its mother for as long as I live…and if there's really a beyond, I'd do anything to have dibs on that, too."

The chagrined look in her eyes faltered. "Well, that only applies if there was actually a…kid. I assure you there is no possibility of one. It's the wrong time completely. So don't worry about that."

He reached for her, pressing her slim but luscious form to his length. "Does this look like a worried man to you?"

She leaned back over his arm, her eyes wary. "This looks like a…high man to me."

"I am. High on you, on the explosively passionate chain reaction we shared." He ground his erection harder into her belly, sensed her ready surrender. "And it's really bad news there isn't a possibility of a kid in there right now. I really, really want to put one in there. Or two. Or more."

Her eyes grew hooded. "What's the rush all of a sudden, about all that life-changing stuff?"

"I don't know." He bent to suckle her earlobe, nip it, before traveling down her neck and lower. "Maybe it's my biological clock. Turning forty does things to a man, y'know?"

She squirmed out of his arms, put a few inches' distance between them. "Since you'll live to a gorgeous, vital hundred, you're not even at the midpoint yet, so chill."

He slammed her back against him. "I don't *want* to chill. I've been chilling in a deep freeze all my life. Now that I've found out what burning in searing passion is like, I'll never want anything else but the scorching of your being. I love you, *ya kanzi,* I more than love you. I adore and worship you. *Ana aashagek.*"

She lurched so hard, she almost broke his hold.

"You—you do?"

He stared into her eyes, a skewer twisting in his gut at what filled them. God, that vulnerability!

Unable to bear that she'd feel that way, he caught her back, holding her in the persuasion of his hands and eyes. "How can you even doubt that I do?"

That precious blush that he'd seen only since last night blazed all over her body. "It's not you I doubt, I guess."

He squeezed her tighter, getting mad at her. "How can you doubt yourself? Are you nuts? Don't you know—"

"How incredible I am? No, not really. Not when it comes to you, anyway. I couldn't even dream that you could have emotions for me. That's why I kept it so strictly chummy. I didn't see how you'd look at me as a woman, thought that I must appear a 'sexless tomboy' to you."

"I was afraid *you* thought you were that. This wasn't how *I* saw you." He filled his hand with her round, firm buttock, pushed the evidence of how he saw her against her hot flesh.

As she undulated against him, her voice thickened. "I was never sexless where you were concerned."

"Don't go overboard now. You were totally so at the beginning. Probably till last night."

Her undulations became languorous, as if he was already inside her, thrusting her to a leisurely rhythm. "If you only knew the thoughts I had where you were concerned."

"And what kind of thoughts were those?"

She rubbed her breasts against him, her nipples grazing against his hair-roughened chest. "Feverishly licentious ones. At least I thought they were. You proved me very uncreative."

He crushed her against him to stop her movements. He had to or he'd be inside her again, and they wouldn't get this out of the way. "If you'd had thoughts of even wanting to hold my hand, you hid them well. Too well, damn it."

Her hands cupped his face, her eyes filling with such tenderness, such remembered pain. "I couldn't risk putting you on edge or having you pull back if you realized

I was just another woman who couldn't resist you. I was afraid it would mar our friendship, that I wouldn't be able to give you the companionship you needed if you started being careful around me. I couldn't bear it if you lost your spontaneity with me."

The fact that she'd held back for him, as he'd done for her, was just more proof of how right they were for one another. "When did you start feeling this way about me?"

"When I was around seventeen."

That flabbergasted him. "But you hated the sight of me!"

"I hated that in spite of all your magnificent qualities you seemed to be just another predictable male who'd go for the prettiest female, no matter that she had nothing more to recommend her. Then I hated that you also seemed so callous—you could be cruel to someone who was so out of your league. But mostly, I hated how you of all men made me feel, when I knew I couldn't even dream of you."

"I beg you, dream of me now," he groaned, burrowing his face into her neck. "Dream of a lifetime with me. Let yourself love me, *ya kanzi.*"

"I far more than love you, Aram. *Ana aashagak kaman.*"

To hear her say she felt the same, *eshg,* stronger than adoration, more selfless than love, hotter than passion, was everything. What he had been born for. For her.

Lowering her onto the bed, he gazed deep into her eyes as she wound herself around him. "I've been waiting for you since I was eighteen. And you had to go get born so much later, make me wait that much longer."

Tears streamed among unbridled smiles. "You can take all the waiting out on me."

Taking her lips, her breath, he pledged, "Oh, I will. How I will."

Floating back to her father's house, Kanza felt like a totally different woman from the one who'd left it over twenty-four hours ago.

She was so high on bliss that she let her family subject her to their drama with a smile. She might have spent three years living autonomously in New York, but once on Zohaydan soil, she must act the unmarried "girl," who could do whatever she wanted during "respectable hours" provided she spent the nights under her father's roof.

To shut them up, she told them of Aram's proposal.

Her news boggled everyone's mind. It seemed beyond their comprehension that she, the one undesirable family member they'd thought would die a spinster, hadn't gotten only one, but two incredible proposals in the space of two days. One from a prince, which she'd dared turn down on the spot, and the other from Aram, someone far bigger and better than any prince. It seemed totally unacceptable to her sisters and stepmothers that she'd marry the incomparable Aram of all men, when *they* had all settled for *far* lesser men.

At least Maysoon was absent, as usual, pursuing her latest escapades outside Zohayd and unconcerned with the rest of her family or their events. Kanza would at least be spared what would have been personal venom, with her history with Aram.

Feeling decidedly Cinderella-like, she thought it was poetic when her prince strolled in. Reading the situation accurately, Aram proceeded to give her family strokes. Showing them he couldn't keep his eyes or hands or even lips off her, he declared he wouldn't wait more than three days for their wedding. A wedding he'd finance from A to Z—unlike her sisters' grooms who divided costs—and that the nuptials would be held at the royal palace of Zohayd.

As her family reeled that Kanza would get a wedding that topped that of a member of the ruling family and in the royal palace, too—where most of them had rarely set foot—Aram took her father aside to discuss her *mahr*. As the dowry or "bride's price" was paid to the father, Aram let everyone hear that her father could name *any* number.

As his *shabkah* to Kanza, the bride's gift, he was writing his main business in her name.

Kanza let him deluge her in extravagant gestures and tumbled deeper in love with him. He was defending her against her family's insensitivity and honoring her in front of them and all of Zohayd by showing them there were no lengths he wouldn't go to for the privilege of her hand.

She'd later tell him that her *mahr* was his heart and her *shabkah* was his body.

But then, he already knew that.

Now that she was as rock-stable certain of his love as he was of hers, she was ready to marry him right there on the spot. Three days felt like such an eternity. Couldn't they just elope?

Kanza really wished they *had* eloped.

Preparing for the wedding, even though Aram had taken care of most of the arrangements, was nerve-racking.

At least now it would be over in a few hours.

If only it would start *already.* The hour until it did felt like forever. Not that anyone else seemed to think so. Everyone kept lamenting that they didn't have more time.

"It's a curse."

Maram, the queen of Zohayd, and Johara's sister-in-law, threw her hands in the air as she turned from sending two of her ladies-in-waiting for last-minute adjustments in Kanza's bridal procession's bouquets. The florist had sent white and yellow roses instead of the cream and pale gold Aram had ordered, which would go with all the gowns.

"No matter what—" Johara explained Maram's exclamation "—we end up preparing royal weddings in less and less time."

Kanza grinned at all the ladies present, still shell-shocked that all the women of the royal houses of Zohayd, Azmahar and even Judar were here to help prepare her wedding. "Take heart, everyone. This is only a *quasi*-royal wedding."

"It is a bona fide royal one around here, Kanza." That was Talia Aal Shalaan, Johara's other sister-in-law. "It's par for the course when you're a friend or relative to any of the royal family members. And you and Aram are both to so many of us. But this is an all-time crunch, and there is no earthshaking cause for the haste as there was in the other royal weddings we've rushed through preparing here."

"Aram can't wait." Johara giggled, winking to her mother, then to Kanza. "That *is* earthshaking."

Talia chuckled. "Another imperious man, huh? He'll fit right in with our men's Brotherhood of Bigheadedness."

Maram pretended severity. "Since this haste is only at his whim, this Aram of yours deserves to be punished."

"Oh, I'll punish him." Kanza chuckled, then blushed as Jacqueline Nazaryan, her future mother-in-law, blinked.

Man, she liked her a lot, but it would be a while until the poised swan of a French lady got used to Kanza's brashness.

Maram rolled her eyes. "And if he's anything like my Amjad, he'll love it. I applaud you for taming that one. I never saw Amjad bristle around another man as he does around Aram. A sign he's in a class of his own in being intractable."

"Oh, Aram is nothing of the sort...." Kanza caught herself and laughed. "*Now.* He told me how he locked horns with Amjad when he lived here, and I think it's because they *are* too alike."

Maram laughed. "Really? Someone who's actually similar to my Amjad? *That* I'd like to see. We might need to put him in a museum."

As the ladies joined in laughter, Carmen Aal Masood came in. Carmen was the event planner extraordinaire whose services Aram had enlisted in return for contributing an unnamed fortune to a few of her favorite charities, and the wife of the eldest Aal Masood brother, Farooq, who gave up the throne of Judar to marry her. The Aal Masoods were also Kanza's relatives from their Aal Ajmaan mother's side.

Yeah, it was all tangled up around here.

"So you ready to hop into your dress, Kanza?" Carmen said, carrying said dress in its wrapping.

Kanza sprang to her feet. "Am I! I can't wait to get this show on the road."

Lujayn, yet another of Johara's sisters-in-law, the wife of Shaheen's half brother Jalal, sighed. "At least you're eager for your wedding to start. Almost every lady here had a rocky start, and our weddings felt like the end of the world."

Farah, the wife of the second-eldest Judarian prince, Shehab Aal Masood, raised her hand. "I had my end of the world *before* the wedding. So I was among the minority who were deliriously happy during it."

"Kanza doesn't seem deliriously happy." Aliyah, King Kamal Aal Masood of Judar's wife—the queen who wore black at her own wedding then rocked the whole region when she challenged her groom to a sword duel on global live feed—gave Kanza a contemplative look. "You're treating it all with the nonchalance of one of the guests. Worse, with the impatience of one of the caterers who just wants it over with so she can get the hell home."

Kanza belted a laugh as she ran behind the screen. "I just want to marry the man. Don't care one bit how I do it."

Feeling the groans of her half sisters flaying her, she undressed and jumped into her gown. They were almost *haybeedo*—going to lay eggs—to have anything like her wedding. And for her to not only have it but to not care about having it must be the ultimate insult to injury to them.

Sighing, she came out from behind the screen.

Her sisters and stepmothers all gaped at her. Yeah, she'd gaped, too, when she'd seen herself in that dress yesterday at the one and only fitting. If you could call it a dress. It was on par with a miracle. Another Aram had made come true.

Before she could get another look at herself in the mirror, the ladies flocked around her, adjusting her hair and veil and embellishing her with pieces of the Pride of Zohayd treasure that King Amjad and Maram were lending her.

Then they pulled back, and it was her turn to gasp.

Who was that woman looking back at her?

The dress's sumptuous gradations of cream and gold made everything about her coloring more vivid, and the incredible amalgam of chiffon, lace and tulle wrapped around her as if it was sculpted on her. The sleeveless, corsetlike, deep décolleté top made her breasts look full and nipped her waist to tiny proportions. Below that, the flare of her hips looked lush in a skirt that hugged them in crisscrossing pleats before falling to the floor in relaxed sweeps. And all over it was embroidered with about every ornament known to humankind, from pearls to sequins to cutwork to gemstones. Instead of looking busy, the amazing subtleness of colors and the denseness and ingeniousness of designs made it a unique work of art. Even more than that. A masterpiece.

Aram had promised he'd tell her how he'd had it made in only two days, if she was very, very, *very* good to him.

She intended to be superlative.

Looking at herself now—with subtle makeup and her thick hair swept up in a chignon that emphasized its shine and volume, with the veil held in place by a crown from the legendary royal treasure, along with the rest of the priceless, one-of-a-kind jewels adorning her throat, ears, arms and fingers—she had to admit she looked stunning.

She wanted to look like that more from now on.

For Aram.

The new bouquets had just arrived when the music that had accompanied bridal processions in the region since time immemorial rocked the palace.

Kanza ran out of the suite with her royalty-studded procession rushing after her, until Johara had to call out for

her to slow down or they'd all break their ankles running
in their high heels.

Kanza looked back, giggling, and was again dumb-
founded by the magnitude of beauty those women packed.
They themselves looked like a bouquet of the most perfect
flowers in their luscious pale gold dresses. Those royal
men of theirs sure knew how to pick women. They had
been blessed by brides who were gorgeous inside and out.

As soon as they were out in the gallery leading to the
central hall, Kanza was again awed by the sheer opulence
of this wonderland of artistry they called the royal palace of
Zohayd. A majestic blend of Persian, Ottoman and Mughal
influences, it had taken thousands of artisans and crafts-
men over three decades to finish it in the mid-seventeenth
century. It felt as if the accumulation of history resonated
in its halls, and the ancient bloodlines that had resided and
ruled in it coursed through its walls.

Then they arrived at the hall's soaring double doors,
heavily worked in embossed bronze, gold and silver Zohaydan motifs. Four footmen in beige-and-gold outfits pulled
the massive doors open by their ringlike knobs. Even over
the music blaring at the back, she heard the buzz of conversation pouring out, that of the thousand guests who'd
come to pay Aram respects as one of the world's premier
movers and shakers.

Inside was the octagonal hall that served as the palace's
hub, ensconced below a hundred-foot high and wide marble dome. She'd never seen anything like it. Its walls were
covered with breathtaking geometric designs and calligra-
phy, its eight soaring arches defining the space at ground
level, each crowned by a second arch midway up, with the
upper arches forming balconies.

At least, that had been what it was when she'd seen it
yesterday. Now it had turned into a scene right out of *Arabian Nights*.

Among the swirling sweetness of *oud,* musk and amber

fumes, from every arch hung rows of incense burners and flaming torches, against every wall breathtaking arrangements of cream and gold roses. Each pillar was wrapped in gold satin worked heavily in silver patterns, while gold dust covered the glossy earth-tone marble floor.

Then came the dozens of tables that were lavishly decorated and set up in echoes of the hall's embellishment and surrounded by hundreds of guests who looked like ornaments themselves, polished and glittering. Everyone came from the exclusive realm of the world's most rich and famous. They sparkled under the ambient light like fairy-tale dwellers in Midas's vault.

Then the place was plunged into darkness. And silence.

Her heart boomed more loudly than the boisterous percussive music that had suddenly ended. After moments of stunned silence, a wildfire of curious murmuring spread.

Yeah. Them and her both. This wasn't part of the planned proceedings. Come to think of it, not much had been. Aram had been supposed to wait at the door to escort her in. She hadn't given it another thought when she hadn't found him there because she'd thought he'd just gotten restless as her procession took forever to get there, and that he'd simply gone to wait for her at the *kooshah,* where the bride and groom presided over the celebrations, keeping the *ma'zoon*—the cleric who'd perform the marriage ritual—company.

So what was going on? What was he up to?

Knowing Aram and his crazy stunts, she expected anything.

Her breathing followed her heartbeat in disarray as she waited, unmoving, certain that there was no one behind her anymore. Her procession had rustled away. This meant they were in on this. So this surprise was for her.

God, she hated surprises.

Okay, not Aram's. She downright adored those, and had,

in fact, gotten addicted to them, living in constant anticipation of the next delightful surprise that invariably came.

But really, now wasn't the time to spring something on
her. She just wanted to get this over with. And get her hands
back on him. Three days without him after that intensive…
initiation had her in a constant state of arousal and frustration. By the end of this torture session, she'd probably
attack and devour him the moment she had him alone.…

"Elli shoftoh, gabl ma tshoofak ainayah.
Omr daye'e. Yehsebooh ezzai alaiah?"

Her heart stopped. Stumbled. Then stopped again.

Aram. His voice. Coming from…everywhere. And he'd
just said…said…

All that I've seen, before my eyes saw you.
A lifetime wasted. How can it even be counted life?

Her heart began ricocheting inside her chest. Aram. Saying exactly what she felt. Every moment before she was with
him, she no longer counted as life.

But those verses… They sounded familiar.…

Suddenly a spotlight burst in the darkness. It took moments until her vision adjusted and she saw…saw…

Aram, rising as if from the ground at the far end of the
gigantic ballroom, among swirling mist. In cream and gold
all over, looking like a shining knight from a fantasy.

As he really was.

Music suddenly rose, played by an orchestra that rose
on a huge platform behind him, wearing complementary
colors.

She recognized the overture. *Enta Omri,* or *You Are My
Lifetime.* One of the most passionate and profound love
songs in the region. That was why the verses had struck
a chord.

Not that their meaning had held any before. Before
Aram, they'd just been another exercise in romantic hy-
perbole. Now that he was in her heart, every word took
on a new meaning, each striking right to her foundations.

He now repeated the verses but not by speaking them. Aram was *singing*. Singing to *her*.

Everything inside her expanded to absorb every nuance of this exquisite moment as it unfolded, to assimilate it into her being.

She already knew he sang well, though it was his voice itself that was unparalleled, not his singing ability. They'd sung together while cooking, driving, playing. He always sang snippets of songs that suited a situation. But nothing local.

While his choice and intention overwhelmed her with gratitude and happiness, the fact that he knew enough about local music to pick this song for those momentous moments stunned her all over again with yet another proof that Aram knew more about her homeland than she did. Not to mention loved it way more.

He was descending the steps from the platform where the orchestra remained. Then he was walking toward her across the huge dance floor on an endless gold carpet flanked by banks of cream rose petals. All the time he sang, his magnificent, soul-scorching voice filling the air, overflowing inside her.

"Ad aih men omri ablak rah, w'adda ya habibi.
Wala da'a el galb ablak farhah wahda.
Wala da'a fel donia ghair ta'am el gerah."
How much of my lifetime before you passed and was lost.
With a heart tasting not a single joy but only wounds.

She shook, tears welling inside her.

Yes, yes. Yes. Exactly. *Oh, Aram...*

He kept coming nearer, his approach a hurricane that uprooted any lingering despondencies and disappointments, blowing them away, never to be seen again.

And he told her, only her, everything in his heart.

"Ebtadait delwa'ti bas, ahheb omri.
Ebtadait delwa'ti akhaf, lal omr yegri."
Only now I started to love my lifetime.

Only now I started to fear its hasty passage.

Every word, everything about him, overwhelmed her. It was impossible, but he was even more beautiful now, from the raven hair that now brushed his shoulders, to the face that had never looked more noble, more potent, every slash carved deeper, every emotion blazing brighter, to the body that she knew from extensive hands-on…investigation was awe incarnate. To make things worse and infinitely better, his outfit showcased his splendor to a level that would have left her speechless, breathless, even without the overkill of his choice of song and his spellbinding performance.

The costume echoed her dress in colors, from the cream-and-gold embroidered cape that accentuated his shoulders and made him look as if he'd fly up, up and away at any moment to the billowing-sleeved gold shirt that was gathered by a cream satin sash into formfitting coordinating pants, which gathered into light beige matte-leather boots.

She was looking at those when he stopped before her, unable to meet his eyes anymore. Her heart had been racing itself to a standstill, needed respite before she gazed up at him and into the full force of his love up close.

His hands reached for her, burned on her bare arms. Quivers became shudders. She raised her eyes, focused on the mike in front of lips that were still invoking the spell.

His hands caressed her face, cupped it in their warmth and tenderness, imbuing her with the purity of his emotions, the power of their union. And he asked her:

"Ya hayat galbi, ya aghla men hayati.
Laih ma abelneesh hawaak ya habibi badri?"
Life of my heart, more precious than my life.
Why didn't your love find me earlier, my love?

Shudders became quakes that dismantled her and dislodged tears from her depths. She waited, heart flailing uncontrollably, for the last verse to complete the perfection.

"Enti omri, elli ebtada b'noorek sabaho."
You are my lifetime, which only dawned with your light.

Music continued in the closing chords, but she no longer heard anything as she hurled herself into his arms.

She rained feverish kisses all over his face, shaking and quaking and sobbing. "Aram…Aram…too much… too much…everything you are, everything with you, from you…" She burrowed into his containment and wept until she felt she'd disintegrate.

He hugged her as if he'd assimilate her, bending to kiss her all over her face, her lips, raggedly reciting the verses, again and again.

She thought a storm raged in the background. It wasn't until she expended her tears and sobs that she realized what it was. The thunder of applause and whistles and hoots among the lightning of camera flashes *and the video flood-lights.*

Drained, recharged, she looked up at her indescribable soul mate, her smile blazing through the upheaval. "This should get record hits on YouTube."

It was amazing, watching his face switch from poignancy to elation to devilry.

Only she could do this to him. As he was the one who could make her truly live.

"Maybe this won't." He winked. "But *this* surely will."

Before she could ask what "this" was, he turned and gestured, and for the second time tonight he managed to stun her out of her wits.

Openmouthed, she watched as hundreds of dancers in ethnic Zohaydan costumes, men in flowing black-and-white robes and women with waist-length hair and in vibrant, intricately embroidered floor-length dresses, poured onto the huge dance floor from all sides, *including* descending by invisible harnesses from the balconies. Drummers with all Zohaydan percussive instruments joined in as they formed facing queues and launched into infectiously energetic local dances.

He caught her around the waist, took her from gravity's

dominion into his. "Remember the dance we learned at that bar in Barbados?" She nodded hard enough to give herself a concussion. He swung her once in the air before tugging her behind him to the dance floor. "Then let's dance, *ya kanzi*."

Though the dance was designed to a totally different rhythm, somehow dancing to this melody worked and, spectacularly, turned out to be even more exhilarating.

Soon all the royal couples were dancing behind them as they led the way, and before long, the whole guest roster had left the tables and were circled around the dance floor clapping or joining the collective dances.

As she danced with him and hugged him and kissed him and laughed until she cried, she wondered how only he could do this—change the way she felt about anything to its opposite. This night she'd wished would be over soon, she suddenly wished would never end.

But even when it did, life with Aram would only begin.

Twelve

Aram clasped Kanza from behind, unable to let her go for even a moment as she handed back the Pride of Zohayd jewelry to the royal guards at the door.

He had to keep touching her to make himself believe this was all real. That she was his wife now. That they were in their home.

Their home.

The fact that it was in Zohayd made it even more unbelievable.

He'd thought he'd lost Zohayd forever. But she'd given it back to him, as she'd given him everything else. Though she'd never loved Zohayd as he loved it, she'd consented to make it her home again.

After seeing her among her family, he now realized why Zohayd had never held fond memories for her. But he was determined to set things right and would put those people in their place. They'd never impact her in any way again.

Now he hoped he could make her see Zohayd as he saw it.

But at any sign of discomfort, they'd leave. He just wanted

her happy, wanted her to have everything. Starting with him and his whole life.

She closed the door then turned and wrapped herself around him. "I just can never predict you."

He tasted her lips, her appreciation. "I hope this keeps me interesting."

Her lips clung to his as she kneaded his buttocks playfully, sensuously. He still couldn't believe, couldn't get enough of how uninhibited she was with him sexually. It was as if the moment he'd touched her she'd let him in all the way, no barriers.

"Don't you dare get more interesting or I'll expire."

"You let me know the level of 'interesting' I can keep that's optimum for your health."

"You're perfect now. You'll always be perfect." She squeezed him tighter. "Thank you, *ya habibi.* For the gift of your song. And every other incredible thing you did and are."

His lips explored her face, loving her so much it was an exquisite pain. "I had to give you a wedding to remember."

"As long as it had you, it would have been the best memory, as everything you are a part of is. *And* it would have been the best possible earthly event. But that…that was divine." Her eyes adored him, devoured him. "Have I told you lately just how out of my mind in love with you I am?"

His heart thundered, unable to wait anymore. He needed union with her. Now.

His hands shook as he undid her dress, slid it off her shoulders. "Last time was ten minutes ago. Too long. Tell me again. *Show* me. You haven't shown me in *three* damn days."

She tore back at his clothes. "Thought you'd never ask."

He shoved off the dress that he'd had ten dressmakers work on day and night, telling himself he couldn't savor her beauty now. He had to lose himself in her, claim her heart, body and soul.

The beast inside him was writhing. This. This flesh. This spirit. This tempest of a woman. Her. It demanded her. And it wouldn't have her slow or gentle. Their lifelong pact had to be sealed in flesh, forged in the fires of urgency and ferociousness. And she wanted that, too. Her eyes were engulfing him whole, her breathing as erratic as his, her hands as rabid as she rid him of his shackles.

He pressed her to the door, crashed his lips down on hers. Her cry tore through him when their mouths collided. He could only grind his lips, his all, against hers, no finesse, no restraint. The need to ram into her, ride her, spill himself inside her, drove him. Incessant groans of profound suffering filled his head, his and hers. He was in agony. Her flesh buzzed its equal torment beneath his burning hands.

He raised her thighs around his hips, growled as her moist heat singed his erection. His fingers dug into her buttocks as he freed himself, pushed her panties out of the way, and her breasts heaved, her hardened nipples branding his raw flesh where she'd torn his shirt off.

Her swollen lips quivered in her taut-with-need face. "Aram…fill me…"

The next moment, he did. He drove up into her, incoherent, roaring, invading her, overstretching her scorching honey. Her scream pierced his soul as she consumed him back, wrung him, razed him.

He rested his forehead against hers, completely immersed in her depths, loved and taken and accepted whole, overwhelmed, transported. He listened to her delirium, watching her through hooded eyes as she arched her graceful back, giving him her all, taking his. Blind, out of his mind and in her power—in her love—he lifted her, filled his starving mouth and hands with her flesh, with the music of her hunger. He withdrew all the way then thrust back, fierce and full, riding her wild cry. It took no more than that. One thrust finished her. And him. Her satin screams echoed his roars as he jetted his essence inside her. Her convulsions spiked with the first splash of his seed against her womb. Her heart hammered under his, both spiraling out of control as the devastating pleasure went on and on and on and the paroxysm of release destroyed the world around them.

Then it was another life. Their new life together, and they were merged as one, rocking together, riding the aftershocks, sharing the descent.

Then, as she always did, she both surprised and delighted him. "That was one hell of an inauguration at the very entrance of our new home. Who needs breaking a bottle across the threshold when you can shatter your bride with pleasure?"

Squeezing her tighter, he looked down at her, his heart soaring at the total satisfaction in her eyes. "I am one for better alternatives."

"That was the *best*. You redefine mind-blowing with every performance. I'm not even sure my head is still in place."

Chuckling, proud and grateful that he could satisfy her that fully, he gathered his sated bride into his arms and strode through the still-foreign terrain of their new home.

Reaching their bedroom suite, he laid her down on the twelve-foot four-poster bed draped in bedcovers the color of her flesh and sheets the color of her hair. She nestled into him and went still, soaking in the fusion of their souls and flesh.

Thankfulness seeped out in a long sigh. "One of the incredible things about your size is that I can bundle you all up and contain you."

She burrowed her face into his chest. "Not fair. I want to contain you, too."

Tightening his arms around her, he pledged, "You have. You do."

* * *

"It is such a relief to be back home in Zohayd."

Kanza looked up from her laptop as Johara waddled toward her, just about to pop.

Johara and her family had returned to Zohayd since her wedding to Aram two months ago. Their stay in New York *had* only been on Aram's account. The moment he'd come to Zohayd, they'd run home.

She smiled at her friend and now new sister-in-law. "I would have never agreed before, but with Aram, Zohayd has become the home it never was to me."

Johara, looking exhausted just crossing their new base of operations, plopped down beside her on the couch. "We knew you'd end up together."

Kanza's smile widened. "Then you knew something I didn't. I had no idea, or even hope, for the longest time."

"Yeah." Johara nodded absently, leafing through the latest status report. "When the situation revolves around you, it's hard to have a clear enough head to see the potential. But Shaheen and I knew you'd be perfect for each other and gave you a little shove."

Her smile faltered. "You did? When was that?"

Johara raised her head, unfocused. Then she blinked. "Oh, the night I sent you to look for that file."

A suspicion mushroomed then solidified into conviction within the same heartbeat. "There was no file, was there?"

Johara gave her a sheepish look. "Nope. I just had to get you both in one place."

Unease stirred as the incident that had changed her life was rewritten. "You sent him to look for the nonexistent file, too, so he'd stumble on me. You set us up."

Johara waved dismissively. "Oh, I just had you meet."

The unease tightened. "Did Aram realize what you did?"

"I'm sure he did when he found you there on his same mission."

So why had he given her different reasons when she'd asked him point-blank what he'd been doing there?

But… "He could have just thought you asked me to do the same thing. He had no reason to think you were setting us up."

"Of course he did. Shaheen had suggested you to him only a couple of weeks before."

"*Suggested* me…how?"

"How do you think? As the most suitable bride for him, of course." Johara's grin became triumphant. "Acting on my suggestion, I might add. And it turns out I was even more right than I knew. You and Aram are beyond perfect."

So their meeting hadn't been a coincidence.

But… "Why should Aram have considered your suggestion? It isn't as if he was looking for a bride."

Johara looked at her as if she asked the strangest things. "Because we showed him what a perfect all-around package you are for him—being you…*and* being Zohaydan. We told him if you married, you'd have each other, he'd have Zohayd back, I'd have my brother back, my parents their son and Shaheen his best friend."

Kanza didn't know how she'd functioned after Johara's blithe revelations.

She didn't remember how she'd walked out of the office or how she'd arrived home. Home. Hers and Aram's. Up until two hours ago, she'd been secure, certain it was. Now…now…

"Kanzi."

He was here. Usually she'd either run to greet him or she'd already be at the door waiting for him.

This time she remained frozen where she'd fallen on the bed, dreading his approach. For what if when he did, when she asked the inevitable questions, nothing would be the same again?

She felt him enter their bedroom, heard the rustle of his

clothes as he took them off. He always came home starving for her, made love to her before anything else, both always gasping for assuagement that first time. Then they settled to a leisurely evening of being best friends and patient, inventive and very, very demanding lovers.

At least, that was what she'd believed.

If everything hadn't started as she'd thought, if his motivations hadn't been as pure as she'd believed them to be, how accurate was her perception of what they shared now?

The bed dipped under his weight, rolling her over to him. He completed the motion, coming half over her as soon as her eyes met his. He'd taken off his jacket and shirt, and he now loomed over her, sculpted by virility gods and unbending discipline and stamina, so hungry and impatient. And her heart almost splintered with doubt and insecurity.

Was it even possible this god among men could truly want her to that extent?

His lips devoured her sob of despair as he rid her of her clothes, sought her flesh and pleasure triggers, cupped the breasts and core that were swollen and aching with the need for him that not even impending heartbreak could diminish.

"Kanza…*habibati…wahashteeni…kam wahashteeni.*"

Her heart convulsed at hearing the ragged emotion in his voice as he called her his love, told her how much he'd missed her. When it had only been hours since he'd left her side.

He slid her pants off her legs, and they fell apart for him. He rose to free his erection, and as she felt it slap against her belly, hot and thick and heavy, everything inside her fell apart, needing his invasion, his affirmation.

Holding her head down to the mattress by a trembling grip in her hair, feeding her his tongue, rumbling his torment inside her, he bathed himself in her body's begging for his, then plunged into her.

That familiar expansion of her tissues at his potency's advance was as always at first unbearable. Then he withdrew and thrust back, giving her more of him, and it got better, then again and again until it was unbearable to have him withdraw, to have him stop. He didn't stop, breaching her to her womb, over and over, until he was slamming inside her with the exact force and speed and depth that would…would…

Then she was shrieking, bucking beneath him with a sledgehammer of an orgasm, the force of it wrenching her around him for every spark of pleasure her body was capable of, wringing him of every drop of his seed and satisfaction.

Before he collapsed on top of her in the enervation of satiation, he as usual twisted around to his back, taking her sprawling on top of him.

Instead of slowing down, her heart hurtled faster until it was rattling her whole frame. It seemed it transmitted to Aram as he slid out of their merging, turned her carefully to her back and rose above her, his face gripped with worry.

"God, what is it, Kanza? Your heart is beating so hard."

And it would stop if she didn't ask. It might shrivel up if she did and got the answers she dreaded.

She had no choice. She had to know.

"Why didn't you tell me that Johara and Shaheen nominated me as a bride for you?"

Thirteen

Kanza's question fell on Aram like an ax.

His first instinct was to deny that he knew what she was talking about. The next second, he almost groaned.

Why had he panicked like that? How could he even consider lying? It was clear Johara or Shaheen or both had told her, but why, he'd never know. But though it wasn't his favorite topic or memory, his reluctance to mention it had resulted in this awkward moment. But that was all it was. He'd pay for his omission with some tongue-lashings, and then she'd laugh off his failure to provide full disclosure about this subject as he did everything else, and that would be that.

He caressed her between the perfect orbs of her breasts, worry still squeezing his own heart at the hammering that wasn't subsiding beneath his palm. "I should have told you."

He waited with bated breath, anticipating the dawning of devilry, the launch of a session of stripping sarcasm.

Nothing came but a vacant, "Yes. You should have."

When that remained all she said and that heart beneath his palm slowed down to a sluggish rhythm, he rushed to qualify his moronically deficient answer. "There was nothing to tell, really. Shaheen made the suggestion a couple of weeks before I met you. I told him to forget it, and that was that."

Another intractable moment of blankness passed before she said, "But Johara set us up that first night. And you must have realized she had. Why didn't you say something then? Or later? When you started telling me everything?"

All through the past months, unease about this omission had niggled at him. He'd started to tell her many times, only for some vague...dread to hold him back.

"I just feared it might upset you."

"Why should it have, if it was nothing? It's not that I think I'm entitled to know everything that ever happened in your life, but this concerned me. I had a right to know."

He felt his skull starting to tighten around his brain. "With the exception of this one thing, I *did* tell you everything in my life. And it was because this concerned you that I chose not to mention it. Their nomination, as well-meaning as it was, was just...unworthy of you."

"But you did act on that nomination. It was why you considered me."

His skull tightened another notch. "No. *No.* I didn't even consider Shaheen's proposition. Okay, I did, for about two minutes. But that was before I saw you that night. If I thought about it again afterward, it was to marvel at how wrong Shaheen was when he thought you'd agree to marry me based on my potential benefits. There's no reason to be upset over this, *ya kanzi.* Johara and Shaheen's matchmaking had nothing to do with us or the soul-deep friendship and love that grew between us."

"Would you have considered me to start with if not for *my* potential benefits?"

"You had none!"

"Ah, but I do. Johara listed them. Stemming from being me and being Zohaydan, as she put it."

"Why the hell would she tell you something like that?

Those pregnancy hormones have been scrambling her brain of late."

"She was celebrating the fact that it all came together so well for all of us, especially you."

"I don't care what she or anyone else thinks. I care about nothing but you. You *know* that, Kanza."

She suddenly let go of his gaze, slipped out of his hold. He watched her with a burgeoning sense of helplessness as she got off the bed, then put on her clothes slowly and unsteadily.

He rose, too, as if from ten rounds with a heavyweight champion, stuffing himself back into his pants, feeling as if he'd been hurled from the sublime heights of their explosively passionate interlude to the bottom of an abyss.

Suddenly she spoke, in that voice that was hers but no longer hers. Expressionless, empty. Dead. "I was unable to rationalize the way you sought me out in the beginning. It was why I was so terrified of letting you close. I needed a logical explanation, and logic said I was nowhere in your league—nothing that could suit or appeal to you."

"You're *everything* that—"

Her subdued voice drowned the desperation of his interjection. "But I was dying to let you get close, so I pounced on Johara's claims that you needed a best friend, then did everything to explain to myself how I qualified as that to you. But her new revelations make much more sense why you were with me, why you married me."

"I was with you because you're everything I could want. I married you because I love you and can't live without you."

"You do appear to love me now."

"*Appear?* Damn it, Kanza, how can you even say this?"

"I can because no matter how much you showed me you loved me, I always wondered *how* you do. *What* I have that the thousands of women who pursued you don't." He again tried to protest the total insanity of her words when lashing pain gripped her face, silencing him more effectively than a skewer in his gut. "When I couldn't find a reason why, I thought you were responding to the intensity of my emotions for you. I thought it was my desire that ignited yours. I did know you needed a home and I thought you found it in me. But your home has always been Zohayd. You just needed someone to help you go home and to have the family and set down the roots you yearned for your entire life."

Unable to bear one more word, he swooped down on her, crushed her to him, stormed her face with kisses, scolding her all the while. "Every word you just said is total madness, do you hear me? You are everything I never dreamed to find, everything I *despaired* I'd never find. I've loved you from that first moment you turned and smacked me upside the head with your sarcasm, then proceeded to reignite my will to exist, then taught me the meaning of being alive."

He cradled her face in his hands, made her look at him. "*B'Ellahi, ya hayati,* if I ever needed your unconditional belief, it's now. My life depends on it, *ya habibati.* I beg you. Tell me you believe me."

Her reddened eyes wavered, then squeezed in consent.

Relief was so brutal his vision dimmed. He tightened his grip on her, reiterating his love.

Then she was pushing away, and alarm crashed back.

Her lips quivered on a smile as she squirmed out of his arms. "I'm just going to the bathroom."

He clung to her. "I'm coming with you."

"It's not that kind of bathroom visit."

"Then call me as soon as it is. There's these new incense and bath salts that I want to try, and a new massage oil."

Her eyes gentled, though they didn't heat as always, as she took another step away. "I'll just take a quick shower."

"Then I'll join you in that. I'll…"

Suddenly the bell rang. And rang.

Since they'd sent the servants away for the night as usual, so they'd have the house and grounds all to themselves, there was no one to answer the door. A door no one ever came to, anyway. So who could this be?

Cursing under his breath as Kanza slipped away, he ran to the door, prepared to blast whoever it was off the face of the earth.

He wrenched the door open, and frustration evaporated in a blast of anxiety when he found Shaheen on his doorstep half carrying an ashen-faced Johara.

He rushed them inside. "God, come in."

Shaheen lowered Johara onto the couch, remained bent over her as Aram came down beside her, each massaging a hand.

"What's wrong? Is she going into labor?"

"No, she's just worried sick," Shaheen said, looking almost sick himself.

Johara clung feebly to the shirt he hadn't buttoned up. "I talked with Kanza earlier, and I think I put my foot in it when I told her how we proposed her to you."

"You *think?*"

At his exclamation, Shaheen glared at him, an urgent head toss saying he wanted a word away from Johara.

Gritting his teeth, he kissed Johara's hot cheek. "Don't worry, sweetheart. It was nothing serious," he lied. "She just skewered me for never mentioning it, and that was it. Now rest, please. Do you need me to get you anything?"

She shook her head, clung to him as he started to rise. "Is it really okay? She's okay?"

He nodded, caressed her head then moved away when she closed her eyes on a sigh of relief.

He joined Shaheen out of her earshot. "God, Shaheen, you shouldn't be letting her around people nowadays. She unwittingly had Kanza on the verge of a breakdown."

Shaheen squeezed his eyes. "*Ya Ullah*... I'm sorry, Aram. Her pregnancy is taking a harder toll on her this time, and I'm scared witless. Her pressure is all over the place and she loses focus so easily. She said she was celebrating how well everything has turned out for you two and only remembered when she came home that Kanza didn't know how things started." He winced. "Then she kept working herself up, recalling how subdued Kanza became during the conversation, the amount of questions she'd asked her, and she became convinced she'd made a terrible mistake."

"She did. God, Shaheen, Kanza kept putting two and two together and getting fives and tens and hundreds. But right before you came she'd calmed down at last."

Hope surged in his friend's eyes. "Then everything is going to be fine?"

He thought her spiraling doubts had been arrested, but he was still rattled.

He just nodded to end this conversation. He needed to get back to Kanza, close that door where he'd gotten a glimpse of hell once and for all.

Shaheen's face relaxed. "Phew. What a close call, eh? Now that that's settled, please tell me when are you going to take my job off my hands? In the past five months since I offered you the minister of economy job, juggling it with everything else—" he tossed a worried gesture in Johara's direction "—has become untenable. I really need you on it right away."

"So this is why you *have* to become Zohaydan."

Kanza's muffled voice startled Aram so much he staggered around. He found her a dozen feet away at the entrance to their private quarters. Her look of pained realization felt like a bullet through his heart.

Her gaze left his, darting around restlessly as if chasing chilling deductions. "Not just to make Zohayd your home, but you need to be Zohaydan to take on such a vital position. But as only members of the ruling house have ever held it, you have to become royalty, through a royal wife."

"Kanza…"

"Kanza…"

Both he and Shaheen started to talk at once.

Her subdued voice droned on, silencing them both more effectively than if she'd shouted. "Since there are no high-ranking princesses available, you had to choose from lower-ranking ones. And in those, I was your only viable possibility. The spinster who never got a proposal, who'd have no expectations, make no demands and pose no challenge or danger. I was your only safe, convenient choice."

He pounced on her, trembling with anxiety and dismay, squeezed her shoulders, trying to jog her out of her surrender to macabre projections. "No, Kanza, hell, *no*. You were the most challenging, *in*convenient person I've ever had the incredible fortune to find."

She raised that blank gaze to his. "But you didn't find me, Aram. You were pushed in my direction. And as a businessman, you gauged me as your best option. Now I know what you meant when you said I 'work best.' For I do. I'm the best possible piece that worked to make everything fall into place without resistance or potential for trouble."

He could swear he could see his sanity deserting him in thick, black fumes. "How can you think, let alone say, *any* of this? After all we've shared?"

Ignoring him, she looked over at Shaheen. "Didn't you rationalize proposing me to him with everything I just said?"

He swung around to order Shaheen to shut up. Every time he or Johara opened their mouths they made things worse.

But Shaheen was already answering her. "What I said was along those lines, but not at all—"

"Why didn't you all just tell me?" Kanza's butchered cry not only silenced Shaheen but stopped Aram's heart. And that was before her agonized gaze turned on him. "I would have given you the marriage of convenience you needed if just for Johara and Shaheen's sake, for Zohayd's. I would have recognized that you'd make the best minister of economy possible, would have done what I could to make it hap-

pen without asking for anything more. But now…now that
you made me hope for more, made me believe I had more—
all of you—I can't go back…and I can't go on."

"Kanza."

His roar did nothing to slow her dash back to the bedroom. It only woke Johara up with a cry of alarm.

Reading the situation at a glance, Johara struggled up
off the couch, gasping, "I'll talk to her."

Unable to hold back anymore, dread racking him, he
shouted, *"No.* You've talked enough for a lifetime, Johara.
I was getting through to her, and you came here to *help* me
some more and spoiled everything."

Shaheen's hand gripped his arm tight, admonishing him
for talking to his sister this way for any reason, and in her
condition. "Aram, get hold of yourself—"

He turned on him. "I *begged* you never to interfere between me and Kanza. Now she might never listen to me,
never believe me again. So *please,* just leave. Leave me to
try to salvage what I can of my wife's heart and her faith
in me. Let me try to save what I can of our marriage, and
our very lives."

Forgetting them as he turned away, he rushed into the
bedroom. He came to a jarring halt when he found Kanza
standing by the bed where they'd lost themselves in each
other's arms so recently, looking smaller than he'd ever
seen her, sobs racking her, tears pouring in sheets down
her suffering face.

He flew to her side, tried to snatch her into his arms. Her
feeble resistance, the tears that fell on his hands, corroded
through to his soul.

Shaking as hard as she was, he tried to hold the hands
that warded him off, moist agony filling his own eyes. "Oh,
God, don't, Kanza…don't push me away, I beg you."

She shook like a leaf in his arms, sobs fracturing her
words. "With everything in me…I do…I *do* want you to
have everything you deserve. I was the happiest person

on earth when I thought that I was a big part of what you need…to thrive, to be happy….”

“You are *everything* I need.”

She shook her head, pushed against him again. “But I’ll always wonder…always doubt. Every second from now on, I’ll look at you and remember every moment we had together and…see it all differently with what I know now. It will…abort my spontaneity, my fantasies…twist my every thought…poison my every breath. *And I can’t live like this.*”

Even in prison, during those endless, hopeless nights when he’d thought he’d be maimed or murdered, he’d never known terror.

But now…seeing and hearing Kanza’s faith, in him—in herself—bleed out, he knew it.

Dark, drowning, devastating.

And he groveled. “No, I beg you, Kanza. I beg you, please…don’t say it. Don’t say it….”

She went still in his arms as if she’d been shot.

That ultimate display of defeat sundered his heart.

Her next words sentenced him to death.

“The moment you get your Zohaydan citizenship and become minister, let me go, Aram.”

Fourteen

It was as harsh a test of character and stamina as Kanza had always heard it was.

But being in the presence of Amjad Aal Shalaan in Kanza's current condition was an even greater ordeal than she'd imagined.

She'd come to ask him as her distant cousin, but mainly as the king of Zohayd, to expedite proclaiming Aram a Zohaydan subject and appointing him to the position of minister.

After the storm of misery had racked her this past week, inescapable questions had forced their way from the depths of despair.

Could she leave Aram knowing that no matter what he stood to gain from their marriage, he did love her? Could she punish him and herself with a life apart because his love wasn't identical to hers, because of the difference in their circumstances?

Almost everyone thought she had far more to gain from their marriage than he did, especially with news spreading of the minister's position. Her family had explicitly expressed their belief that marrying him would raise her to undreamed-of status and wealth.

But she expected him to believe she cared nothing about those enormous material gains, to know for certain that they were only circumstantial. She would have married him had he been destitute. She would continue to love him, come what may. So how could she not believe him when he said the same about his own projected gains? Could she impose a separation on both of them because her ego had been injured and her confidence shaken?

No. She couldn't.

Even if she'd never be as certain as she'd been before the revelations, she would heal and relegate her doubts to the background, where they meant nothing compared to truly paramount matters.

Once she had reached that conclusion, she'd approached a devastated Aram and tried everything to persuade him that he must go ahead with his plans, to persuade him that she'd overreacted and was taking everything she'd said back.

He'd insisted he'd *never* had plans, didn't want anything but her and would never lift a finger to even save his life if it meant losing her faith and security in the purity of his love.

So here she was, taking matters into her own hands.

She was getting him what he needed, what he was now forgoing to prove himself to her.

Not that she seemed to be doing a good job of championing his cause.

That cunning, convoluted Amjad had been keeping her talking for the past half hour. It seemed he didn't buy the story that she wished Aram to be Zohaydan as soon as possible for the job's sake…that Shaheen needed Aram to take over before Johara gave birth.

He probed her with those legendary eyes of his, confirmed her suspicion. "So, Kanza, what's your *real* rush? Why do you want your husband to become Zohaydan so immediately? He can assume Shaheen's responsibilities without any official move. I'd prefer it, to see if my younger brother wants to hand his closest friend the kingdom's fate as a consolation prize for the 'lost years,' or if he is really the best man for the job."

"He is that, without any doubt."

Those eyes that were as vividly emerald as Aram's were azure flashed their mockery. "And of course, that's not the biased opinion of a woman whose head-over-heels display during her wedding caused my eyes to roll so far back in my skull it took weeks to get them back into their original position?"

"No, *ya maolai*." It was a struggle to call him "my lord," when all she wanted to do was chew him out and make him stop tormenting her. "It's the very objective opinion of a professional in Aram's field. While there's no denying that you, Shaheen and your father have been able to achieve great things running the ministry, I believe with the unique combination of his passion for the job and for Zohayd, and with the magnitude of his specific abilities and experience, Aram would surpass your combined efforts tenfold."

Amjad's eyebrows shot up into the hair that rained across his forehead. "Now, *that's* a testimony. I might be needing your ability to sell unsellable goods quite soon."

"As reputedly the most effective king Zohayd has ever known, I hear you've achieved that by employing only the best people where they'd do the most good. I trust you wouldn't let your feelings for Aram, whatever they are, interfere with the decision to make use of him where he is best suited."

He spread his palm over his chest in mock suffering. "Ah, my feelings for Aram. Did he tell you how he broke my heart?"

You, too? she almost scoffed.

Not that Aram had broken hers. It was she who'd churned herself out with her insecurities.

But that big, bored regal feline would keep swatting her until she coughed up an answer he liked.

She tried a new one. "I'm pregnant."

And she was.

She'd found out two days after Johara's revelations. She hadn't told Aram.

"I want Aram to be Zohaydan before our baby comes."

Amjad raised one eyebrow. "Okay. Good reason. But again, what's the rush? Looking at you, I'd say you have around seven months to go. And you seem to want this done last week."

"I need Aram settled into his new job and his schedule sorted out with big chunks of time for me and the baby."

"Okay. Another good reason. Want to add a better one?"

"I haven't told Aram he's going to be a father yet. I wish him to be Zohaydan before I do to make the announcement even more memorable."

His bedeviling inched to the next level. "You have this all figured out, haven't you?"

"Nothing to figure out when you're telling the truth."

Those eyes said "liar." Out loud he said, "You're tenacious and wily, and you're probably making Aram walk a tightrope to keep in your favor...."

"Like Queen Maram does with you, you mean?"

He threw his head back on a guffaw. "I like you. But even more than that, you must be keeping that pretty, pretty full-of-himself Aram in line. I like *that*."

"Are we still talking about Aram, *ya maolai?*"

His cruelly handsome face blazed with challenge and enjoyment. "And she can keep calling me *ya maolai* with a straight face, right after she as much as said, 'I'd put you over my knee, you entitled brat, if I possibly could.'"

Even though he didn't seem offended in the least by the subtext of her ill-advised retort, the worry that she might end up spoiling Aram's chances was brakes enough.

"I thought no such thing, *ya maolai.*"

He hooted. "Such a fantastic liar. And that gets you extra

points. Now let's see if you can get a gold star. Tell me the real reason you're here, Kanza."

Nothing less would suffice for this mercilessly shrewd man who had taken one of the most internally unstable kingdoms in the region, brought it to heel and was now leading it to unprecedented prosperity.

So she gave him the truth. "Because I love Aram. So much it's a constant pain if I can't give him everything he needs. And he *needs* a home. He needs *Zohayd*. It's part of his soul. It *is* his home. But until it is that for real, he'll continue to feel homeless, as he's felt for far too long. I don't want him to feel like that one second longer."

Amjad narrowed his eyes. He was still waiting. He knew there was just a bit more to the truth, damn him.

And she threw it in. "I didn't want to expose his vulnerability to you of all people, to disadvantage him in this rivalry you seem to have going."

His lips twisted. "You don't consider this rivalry would be moot and he'd be in a subordinate position once he becomes a minister in my cabinet, in a kingdom where I'm king?"

"No. On a public, professional level, Aram would always hold his own. No one's superior office, which has nothing to do with skill or worth, would disadvantage him. But I was reluctant to hand you such intimately personal power over him. I do now only because I trust you won't abuse it."

It seemed as if he gave her a soul and psyche scan, making sure he'd mined them for every last secret he'd been after.

Seemingly satisfied that he had, Amjad flashed her a grin. "Good girl. That took real guts. Putting the man you love at my mercy. And helluva insight, too. Because I am now bound by that honor pact you just forced on me to never abuse my power over your beloved, I'm definitely going to be making use of this acumen and power of persuasion of yours soon. And as your gold star, you get your wish."

Her heart boomed with relief.

He went on. "Just promise you will not be too good to Aram. You'd be doing him a favor exercising some...*severe* love. Otherwise his head will keep mushrooming, when it's already so big it's in danger of breaking off his neck."

She rose, gave him a tiny bow. "I will consult with Queen Maram about the best methods of limiting the cranial expansion of pretty, pretty full-of-themselves paragons, *ya maolai.*"

His laugh boomed.

She could hear him still laughing until she got out of hearing range. The moment she was, all fight went out of her.

This had been harder than she'd thought it would be.

But she'd done it. She'd gotten Aram the last things he needed. Now to convince him that it wouldn't mean losing her.

For though she was no longer secure in the absoluteness of his need for her, and only her, she'd already decided that anything with him would always remain everything she needed.

Amjad did far better than she'd expected.

The morning after her audience with him, he sent her a royal decree. It proclaimed that in only six hours, a ceremony would be held at the royal palace to pronounce her husband Zohaydan. And to appoint him as the new minister of economy.

She flew to Aram's home office and found him just sitting on the couch, vision turned inward.

The sharp, ragged intake of breath as she came down on his lap told her he'd been so lost in his dark reverie he hadn't noticed her entrance. Then as she straddled him, the flare of vulnerability, of entreaty in his eyes, made ever-simmering tears almost burst free again.

Ya Ullah, how she loved him. And she'd starved for him.

She hadn't touched him since that night, unable to add passion to the volatile mix. He hadn't tried to persuade her again. Not because he didn't want to. She knew he did. He'd gone instantly hard between her legs now, his arousal buffeting her in waves. He'd been letting her guide him into what she'd allow, what she'd withstand.

She'd show him that for as long as he wanted her, she was his forever. That he was her everything.

She held his beloved head in her hands, moans of anguish spilling from her lips as they pressed hot, desperate kisses to his eyes, needing to take away the hurt in them and transfer it into herself. He groaned with every press, long and suffering, and remorse for the pain she'd caused him during her surrender to insecurity came pouring out.

"I'm sorry, Aram. Believe me, please. I *didn't* mean what I said. It was my insecurities talking."

He threw his head back on the couch, his glorious hair fanning to frame his haggard face. "*I'm* sorry. And you had every right to react as you did."

She pressed her lips to his, stopping him from taking responsibility. She wanted this behind them. "No, I didn't. And you have nothing to be sorry about."

His whole face twisted. "I just am. So cripplingly sorry that you felt pain on my account, no matter how it happened."

She kissed him again and again. "Don't be. It's okay."

"No, it's not. I can't bear your uncertainty, *ya habibati.* I can't breathe, I can't *be*...if I don't have your belief and serenity. I'd die if I lost you."

"I'm never going anywhere. I was being stupid, okay? Now quit worrying. You have more important things to worry about than my insecurities."

"I worry about nothing but what you think and feel, *ya kanzi.* Nothing else is important. Nothing else even matters."

"Then you have nothing to worry about. Since only

you…only us, like *this*…matters to me, too." Her hands feverishly roved over him, undoing his shirt, his pants. She rained bites and suckles over his formidable shoulders and torso, releasing his daunting erection. A week of desolation without him, knowing that his seed had taken root inside her, made the ache for him uncontrollable, the hunger unstoppable.

But it was clear he wouldn't take, wouldn't urge. He'd sit there and let her do what she wanted to him, show him what she needed…take all she wanted. And she couldn't wait.

She shrugged off her jacket, swept her blouse over her head, snapped off her bra and bunched up her skirt. She rose to her knees to offer him her breasts, to scale his length. He devoured her like a starving man, reiterating her name, his love.

Her core flowed as she pushed aside her panties then sank down on him in one stroke. Her back arched at the shock of his invasion. Sensations shredded her. *Aram.* Claiming her back, taking her home. Her only home.

She rose and fell over him, their mouths mating to the same rhythm of their bodies. He forged deeper and deeper with every plunge, each a more intense bolt of stimulation. She'd wanted it to last, but her body was already hurtling toward completion, every inch of him igniting the chain reaction that would consume her.

As always, he felt her distress and instinctively took over, taking her in his large palms, lifting her, thrusting her on that homestretch to oblivion until the coil of need broke, lashing through her in desperate surges of excruciating pleasure.

"Aram, *habibi,* come with me…."

He let go at her command, splashing her walls with his essence. And she cried out her love, her adoration, again and again. *"Ahebbak, ya hayati, aashagak."*

Aram looked up at Kanza as she cried out and writhed the last of her pleasure all over him, wrung every drop of his from depths he'd never known existed before collapsing over him, shuddering and keening her satisfaction.

She'd taken her sentence back, had again expunged his record, giving him the blessing of continuing as if nothing had happened. She'd called him her love and life again. She'd made soul-scorching love to him.

So why wasn't he feeling secure that this storm was over?

She was stirring, her smile dawning as she let him know she wanted to lie down.

Maneuvering so she was lying comfortably on her side on the couch, he got her the jacket she reached for. She fished an envelope from its pocket. At its sight, his heart fisted.

He recognized the seal. The king of Zohayd's. He was certain what this was.

With a radiant smile, she foisted it on him. And sure enough, it was what he'd expected. She'd gone and gotten him everything that just a week ago she'd thought he'd married her to get.

And she'd made love to him before presenting it to him to reassure him that accepting this wouldn't jeopardize their relationship. She was giving him everything she believed he needed. Zohayd as his home. The job that would be the culmination of his life's work, putting him on par with the ruling family.

He again tried to correct her assumptions about his needs. "I need only you, *ya kanzi*...."

"How many times will I tell you I'm okay now? I just showed you how okay I was."

"But we still need to talk."

She kissed him one last time before sitting up. "And we will. As much as you'd like. After the ceremony, okay? Just forget about everything else now."

Could *she* forget it, or would she just live with it? When she'd said before that she couldn't?

He feared *that* might be the truth. That she was just giving in to her love, her need for him, but even more, his love and need for her. But in her heart, she'd never regain her total faith in him, her absolute security in his love.

"Let's get you ready," she said as she pulled him to his feet. "This is the most important day of your life."

"It certainly isn't. That day is every day with you."

She grinned and he saw his old Kanza. "Second most important, then. Still pretty important if you ask me. C'mon, Shaheen said he'd send you the job's 'trimmings.'"

He'd always known she was one in a million, that he'd beaten impossible odds finding her. But what she was doing now, the extent to which she loved him, showed him how impossibly blessed he was.

And he was going to be worthy of her miracle.

Aram glanced around the ceremony hall.

It looked sedate and official, totally different than it had during his and Kanza's fairy-tale wedding. The hundreds present today were also dressed according to the gravity of the situation. This was the first time in the past six hundred years that a foreigner had been introduced into the royal house and had taken on one of the kingdom's highest offices.

As Amjad walked into the hall with his four brothers behind him, Aram stole a look back at Kanza. His heart swelled as she met his eyes, expectant, emotional, proud.

What had he done so right he'd deserved to find her? An angel wouldn't deserve her.

But he would. He'd do everything and anything to be worthy of her love.

Amjad now stood before his throne, with his brothers flanking him on both sides. Shaheen was to his right. He met Aram's eyes, his brimming with pride, pleasure, excitement and more than a little relief.

Aram came to stand before the royal brothers, in front

of Amjad, who wasn't making any effort to appear solemn, meeting his eyes with his signature irreverence.

Giving back as good as he got, he repeated the citizenship oath. But as he kneeled to have Amjad touch his head with the king's sword while reciting the subject proclamation, Amjad gave him what appeared to be an accidental whack on the head—intentionally, he was certain.

Aram rose, murmuring to Amjad that it was about time they did something about their long-standing annoyance with each other. Amjad whimsically told him he wished he could oblige him. But he'd promised Kanza he'd share his lunch with him in the playground from now on.

Pondering that Kanza had smoothed his path even with Amjad, he accepted the citizenship breastpin.

Yawning theatrically, Amjad went through the ritual of proclaiming him the minister of economy, pretending to nod off with the boredom of its length. Then it was the minister's breastpin's turn to join the other on Aram's chest. This time, Amjad made sure he pricked him.

Everyone in the hall rose to their feet, letting loose a storm of applause and cheers. He turned to salute them, caught Kanza's smile and tearful eyes across the distance. Then he turned back to the king.

In utmost tranquility, holding Amjad's goading gaze, he unfastened the breastpins one by one, then, holding them out in the two feet between them, he let them drop to the ground.

The applause that had faltered as he'd taken the breastpins off came to an abrupt halt. The moment the pins clanged on the ground, the silence fractured on a storm of collective gasps.

Aram watched as Amjad shrewdly transferred his gaze from Kanza's shocked face back to his.

Then that wolf of a man drawled, "So did my baby brother not explain the ritual to you? Or are you taking off your sharp objects to tackle me to the ground here and now?"

"I'll tackle you in the boardroom, Amjad. And I know exactly what casting the symbols of citizenship and status to the ground means. That I renounce both, irrevocably."

Amjad suddenly slapped him on the shoulder, grinning widely. "What do you know? You're not a stick-in-the-mud like your best friend. If you're as interesting as this act of madness suggests you are, I might swipe you from him."

"Since you did this for me to please Kanza, you're not unsalvageable yourself, after all, Amjad. Maybe I'll squeeze you in, when I'm not busy belonging to Kanza."

"Since I'm also busy belonging to Maram, we'll probably work a reasonable schedule. Say, an hour a year?"

Suddenly liking the guy, he grinned at him. "You're on."

As he turned around, Shaheen was all over him, and Harres, Haidar and Jalal immediately followed suit, scolding, disbelieving, furious.

He just smiled, squeezed Shaheen's shoulder then walked back among the stunned spectators and came to kneel at Kanza's feet. Looking as if she'd turned to stone, she gaped down at him, eyes turbid and uncomprehending.

He took her hands, pulled her to his embrace. "The only privileges I'd ever seek are your love and trust and certainty. Would you bestow them on me again, whole, pure and absolute? I can't and won't live without them, *ya kanzi*."

And she exploded into action, grabbing him and dragging him behind her among the now-milling crowd.

"Undo this!"

Amjad turned at her imperative order, smiling sardonically. "No can do. Seems this Aram of yours *is* too much like me, poor girl. He's as crazy as I am."

She stamped her foot in frustration. "You *can* undo this. You're the king."

Amjad tsked. "And undo *his* grand gesture? Don't think so."

"So you can undo it!" she exclaimed.

Amjad shook his head. "Sorry, little cousin. Too many pesky witnesses and tribal laws. Your man knew exactly what he was doing and that it cannot be undone. But let me tell you, it makes him worthy of you. That took guts, and also shows he knows exactly what works for him, what's worthy. *You.* So just enjoy your pretty, pretty full-of-himself guy's efforts to worship you."

She looked between him and Amjad in complete and utter shock. "But…what will Shaheen do when Johara gives birth? What about Zohayd…"

"The only world that would collapse without your Aram is yours. And I guess that's why he's doing this. To make it—" Amjad winked at her "—impregnable."

As she continued to argue and plead, Aram swept her up in his arms and strode out of the palace, taking her back home.

Her protests kept coming even after he'd taken her home and made love to her twice.

He rose on his elbow, gathered her to him. "I'll work the job as if I'd taken the position, so I won't leave Shaheen in the lurch. All that'll be missing is the title, which I care nothing about. I want the work itself, the achievement. But contrary to what Shaheen said, I don't need to be always in Zohayd or need to belong here. I already belong. With you, to you."

She wound herself around him, inundating him with her love, which, to his eternal relief, was once again unmarred by uncertainty and fiercer than ever before. "You didn't have to do it. I would have gotten over the last traces of insecurity in a few weeks tops."

"I wouldn't leave you suffering uncertainty for a few minutes. You are more than my home, *ya kanzi.* You're my haven. You contain me whole, you ward off my own demons and anything else the world could throw at me. I haven't lost a thing, and I have gained everything. I *have* everything. Because I have you."

She threw herself at him again before pulling back to look at him with shyness spreading over that face that was his whole world.

"And you're going to have more of me. Literally. And in seven months I'll give you a replica of you."

He keeled over her. As she shrieked in alarm, he laughed, loud and unfettered, then kissed her breathless, mingling their tears.

A baby. There was no end to her blessings.

After yet another storm of rapture passed, he said, "I want a replica of *you*."

"Sorry, buddy, it'll be your replica. In Zohayd they say the baby looks like the parent who is loved more. Uh-uh-uh…" She silenced him as he protested. "I've loved you longer, so you can't do a thing about it. So there."

"I trust this applies only to the first baby. The second one doesn't follow those rules. Second one, your replica."

"But I want them all disgustingly pretty like you!"

He pounced on her, and soon the laughter turned to passion, then to delirium, frenzy and finally pervasive peace.

And through it all, he gave thanks for this unparalleled treasure, this hurricane who'd uprooted him from his seclusion and tossed him into the haven of her unconditional love.

* * * * *

If you liked Kanza and Aram, check out
TEMPORARILY HIS PRINCESS,
the first MARRIED BY ROYAL DECREE *novel,*
available now!

And look for more novels
in USA TODAY *bestselling author*
Olivia Gates's series
MARRIED BY ROYAL DECREE*!*

If you loved the drama and sensuality of
USA TODAY *bestselling author Olivia Gates*
then don't miss CLAIMING HIS OWN,
a BILLIONAIRES AND BABIES *story,*
coming November 2013!

COMING NEXT MONTH FROM

HARLEQUIN®

Desire

Available October 1, 2013

#2257 YULETIDE BABY SURPRISE

Billionaires and Babies • by Catherine Mann

The holiday spirit has professional rivals Mariama and Rowan caring for an abandoned baby—together. But when playing house starts to feel all too real, will they say yes to becoming a family?

#2258 THE LONE STAR CINDERELLA

Texas Cattleman's Club: The Missing Mogul
by Maureen Child

With her boss missing, housekeeper Mia needs a new gig. What she gets is a makeover, a job posing as cattleman Dave Firestone's fiancée—and a chance at a fairy-tale ending?

#2259 A BEAUTY UNCOVERED • *Secrets of Eden*

by Andrea Laurence

When brazen beauty Samantha starts working for beastly CEO Brody Eden, she's determined to tame him. But to capture his heart she must also heal him body and soul....

#2260 A WOLFF AT HEART

The Men of Wolff Mountain • by Janice Maynard

Switched at birth? Pierce Avery must know, so he hires Nicola to uncover the truth—only to find he needs *her*...until she digs up a secret that could tear them apart.

#2261 A COWBOY'S TEMPTATION

Colorado Cattle Barons • by Barbara Dunlop

Rancher-turned-mayor Seth Jacobs wants a railroad in the valley, but a sexy resort owner proves a very tempting roadblock. He'll convince her to relocate...and then he'll have her in his bed.

#2262 COUNTERING HIS CLAIM • by Rachel Bailey

Inheriting *half* a cruise liner is not what hotelier Luke Marlow expected. But to own it all, he'll have to navigate the waters with his new partner— the unsuspecting and sexy on-board doctor.

HDCNM0913